SHADOWED DESIRES

BY

KALI WILLOWS

Featuring...

Double Dragon Seduction
Damnation & Desire
Designing Passion
Terminal Lust
Savannah's Ghost Tale

ငဃ

Decadent Publishing Company
www.decadentpublishing.com

Shadowed Desires
Copyright 2012 by Kali Willows
ISBN: 978-1-61333-282-5
Cover art by LFD and Cribley Designs

Published by Decadent Publishing Company

Look for us online at:
www.decadentpublishing.com

Printed in the United States of America

Dedication

To my faithful readers; without you, I would have no inspiration,
& to the wonderful folks of Decadent Publishing, for their dedication and the positive atmosphere they strive to create for their authors!

The creators of the 1Night Stand Series had a good feeling about it when they began, but they had no idea how endless and inspirational Madame Evangeline's match making abilities would be for the multitude of authors drawn into her magical pull. A pull to which Kali was powerless.

Teasers

Double Dragon Seduction
Urban fantasy/paranormal/erotic romance/interracial – (m/f/m)/ménage

Heat Level - 5

Gwen Trembley is disturbed with the upcoming wedding of her reprehensible ex, and coping with her emerging dark side with a surprising talent. Years of suppressed sexuality prompts her unyielding need for an extraordinary experience. Gwen seeks the services of 1NS for a night where new carnal knowledge will revive her damaged soul. Madame Eve has the perfect arrangements, but perhaps twice what she bargained for.

Twin brothers Tatsu and Yong Li are in desperate need of a unique woman who can accept them as inseparable. They carry not one, but two inconceivable secrets. These exotic brothers can't be with just any woman, and any who dare try, will find themselves facing the most passionate, lust-filled night of their lives, but will she survive? More so, will they? 1NS finds a match they never expected possible.

"Double Dragon Seduction was an emotionally packed, complicated story, with a unique mythology."
~ Sizzling Hot Books

Damnation & Desire
Paranormal/erotic romance – (m/f)

Heat level - 4

A Wiccan descendent of a notorious victim of the Salem witch trials, Tessa Ledger is obsessed with the Malleus Maleficarum and its claim that women are susceptible to the influence of the devil through their sexuality. Tessa seeks the services of 1Night Stand to tame her blazing carnal desires, and perform a little experiment on bewitching men. Her date is to take place in Salem...on the most supernatural night possible, where the veil between the living and the dead is at its thinnest and anything can happen.

Samson Langley is a highly revered clergyman in a small town near Salem. Being a positive community leader and overcoming his ancestral legacy has been his lifelong purpose, but his natural urges plague him night and day. With a few qualms, he agrees to his mentor's suggestion to exorcise his personal demons with a date arranged by Madame Evangeline of 1Night Stand. He doesn't expect to find his own faith and integrity in question as he is faced with satisfaction, or damnation in the arms of a one-night stand.

"As you can imagine, the pairing of a witch and a man of the cloth presents some conflict. The plot was quite good, very developed..." ~ Sizzling Hot Books

Designing Passion
Contemporary/erotic romance (m/f)
Heat level - 4

Fifteen years ago, Tawny Reeve was in love, but her wealthy, jet-setting parents went to cruel lengths to separate her from her middle class lover. Emotionally barren, she despairs of ever finding love again. A friend sent her an email address with only a name in the subject line: "Madame Evangeline". Tawny doubts she is capable of a normal, loving relationship, but maybe she can handle a one-night stand, at least meeting her body's needs, if not her heart's.

Wyatt Mackenzie is an accomplished architect with a lonely lifestyle. None of the debutantes and gorgeous women he dates have brought him the electrifying passion he hopes to rekindle from his youth. There was only one who captured his heart, and then smashed it into a thousand pieces. An email from his client at the Castillo hotel in Vegas, offers a solution to his passionless life: "Email Madame Evangeline, and she can make your wildest dreams come true."

"— the setting is exotic and the sex scenes hot... and the conclusion more than satisfying..." ~The Long and Short Of It Reviews

"A strong plot with a sweet romance building to a heated night of lovin', Ms Willows gives us a short story to remember." ~Cathyr (Australia)

Terminal Lust

Urban fantasy/paranormal/erotic romance (m/f)
Heat level – 4

Ambrosia Thatcher is a woman with little time and a single wish; *to experience passion once more.* She's been given a death sentence. Seeking answers to her unbearable paralysis at three thirty three, every single morning, the enlightenment she is offered holds no solace, not from the ramblings of a crazy old gypsy. The services of 1NS is the only prescription to cure her longing for passion, but will she survive long enough to see it through?

Desmond Jacobs is an immortal haunted by the very woman he cannot find. The prospect of eternal seclusion without her has no appeal, so he has a plan. With the aid of his creator, he will to go to sleep, and never wake up again. Despite his determination, he agrees to one last request from his friend; *seek the services of 1NS to find another.* Which will overpower him first; his hunger for sexual healing or his thirst for blood?

"Kali Willows does it again! She writes such wonderful characters that you really get invested with

6

them... Bravo Kali!" ~Night Owl Reviews

"Terminal Lust is a gripping tale ...The passion was exciting and erotic, the characters sizzle and steam up the pages ..." ~Sizzling Hot Books

Savannah's Ghost Tale
Paranormal /erotic romance (m/f)
Heat level - 4

Savannah Teale has an obsession with the supernatural—to disprove it. An unorthodox Ghost Hunter with a dark secret, she doesn't believe in life after death. Not anymore. Being romantically challenged since the traumatic death of her fiancé, she has no interest in dating, but her sister's loving interference has led her to accept a date for a 1Night Stand.

Cameron Evans is one of Savannah's most handsome, charismatic, and sexy bachelors. He's an exceptionally gifted tour guide, and a psychic, but hasn't learned how to turn off his gifts. Since his conversations with the dead are a turn-off for most women—to put it mildly—Cameron has turned to Madame Eve to find a woman who can accept him for himself and all he has to give. They may be a great match—if certain, lingering ghost would just step out of the picture.

"...a fantastic twist on a traditional ghost story... there is something just so genuine about their interactions. The setting of this story is fabulous and almost takes on a life of its own, as if it were a main character..." ~Got Erotic Romance Review

DOUBLE DRAGON SEDUCTION

BY

KALI WILLOWS

Chapter One

Mr. Jamison Trembley and his fiancé, Katrina Harlan, will exchange wedding vows at her parents' estate in Niagara Falls on the eve of December first.

The doorbell startled her and she wobbled on the high kitchen stool. A wave of hatred flooded her and the newspaper burst into flame in her hands. She dropped it on the floor then extinguished it with her slipper.

The shrill chime sounded again.

"Yeah, yeah, I'm coming already."

Gwen peeked through the side window curtain then grinned and opened the door. "Hey." She spun and headed back toward the kitchen.

"So, I guess I'm too late?" Cindy joined her.

"You are? For what?" Resuming her seat at the island, she drummed her nails in irritation.

Cindy stepped over the pile of smoldering ashes and grimaced. "I was hoping to steal your paper before you found it." She pulled two glasses and a bottle of amaretto from the cabinet, poured double shots, and handed one to Gwen.

"Even if you had, you couldn't stop the gossip." She gulped back the sweet liqueur and slammed the tumbler down, wishing for another.

"Subtlety has never been his strong point." Cindy sucked back her own shot.

"No...it isn't."

"Getting married on your birthday, though, that's low, even for him. What an asshole."

"Cheers to that."

℃

An hour, and three quarters of the bottle later, Gwen sat beside Cindy on the leather couch in her den, staring at the sputtering flames of oak in the fireplace. She tried to let the soft crackling, and dark shadows dancing across the walls and ceiling soothe her—with minimal success.

"So, what are you gonna do, sunshine?" Cindy's sympathetic tone grated on Gwen's nerves, as did her practical message. "He's clearly moved on. Are you ready to let go?"

The liquid pain killer was kicking in, smoothing the rough edges of her anger and grief. "I have no idea what to do. I mean, ten years together—how do I just give that up?"

"If you could take him back, would you?"

She gasped. "Are you crazy?"

"No, but I would have thought *you* were, if you wanted him back." Cindy tucked a leg under her and faced Gwen.

"I know I'm better off without him, but it doesn't make it any easier, you know?" She hated the tears that choked her voice.

"Yeah, I understand, but one day soon, you'll discover something I've known about you all along."

"What's that?"

"You're stronger than you think. Look what you've survived." Cindy reached over and patted her hand. "You're amazing, and I'm proud of you."

Avoiding her friend's eyes, she propped her feet on the glass table, knocking a pile of books over.

"I got it." Cindy laughed and collected them from the floor. "I can see what you *have* been doing lately. How much time have you been spending reading this smut?" She held up a book with a demon and angel illustration on the cover, the blurb touting a lurid tale of erotic passion.

"Gimme that." Gwen grabbed it.

"No wonder you're depressed, reading all these... these... romances with monsters?"

"I read it *because I'm depressed.* I need something to distract me while he's living it up with that slut."

"But it's just fantasy. None of it's real."

"That's the beauty of it, Cin. If you know it can't be real, you don't get caught up with the roses and champagne, the farce of *what real love could be,* blah, blah, blah."

"Honey," Cindy reached for the book, but Gwen pulled away, clutching it to her chest like a life preserver.

"Leave me my fantasies. They're not real anyway." She lifted her chin. It was little enough to ask, after all.

"Whatever works for you, sweetie." Cindy's gaze softened as she reclined into her seat.

"Joshua, the hero of the story, may be a demon, but at least *he* has a soul, unlike that selfish bastard."

"Okay." Cindy snickered. "No need to get pissy. I get it."

"Even though it's fiction, can you imagine what being with a supernatural creature would be like?" Gwen's fingers teased the smooth, glossy cover as she allowed her intimate imaginings to slip out.

"What do you mean?" Cindy sipped her drink, watching her with a frown.

"Well, how hot is this?" She opened the book. *"His wings encompassed her trembling body as he descended upon her quivering lips."*

"Wings? Oh come on."

"Don't get your panties in a bunch." Gwen flashed her an evil grin.

"What?"

"I did get inspired after we spoke last week." Bursting inside, she couldn't keep her secret any longer. "I heard about a dating service." She dropped into her office chair and booted up her laptop, anxious to share her find.

"Dating service? Have you lost your mind?" Cindy joined her, looking over her shoulder at the monitor. "You said you didn't want a relationship right now."

"True, but I never said I didn't want an outlet for my pent-up frustrations." She logged into email and reveled in the sense of empowerment, the first positive emotion she'd experienced in a while.

Cindy dragged a chair next to hers and sat down, peering at the screen.

"What do you mean?"

"Madame Evangeline found a match for me, for an *extraordinary night* that has nothing to do with an average man, a selfish man, an ass—"

"Okay, open it." Cindy grabbed for the mouse.

"My, my, aren't we nosey?" Gwen taunted. "Listen. *At your request, we have reviewed your application and found a suitable match for your 1Night Stand.*"

"Oh, my God, anonymous sex? You?" Cindy's jaw hung open.

"It gets even better, my dear."

"What?" Cindy took a sip of her drink.

"I didn't ask to be with a man."

Cindy choked. "Holy crap, I thought you were totally straight." She arched a brow. "Next time you drop a bomb like that, wait until I'm done taking a drink. That came out my nose."

"Sorry about that," Gwen giggled. "I'm not seeking a *woman.*"

"I'm confused. You're gonna have sex, but not with a man, and not with a woman?"

"Oh, I'll be seeing a man—actually; I'll be seeing two of them."

"Two guys?"

"Yep." She grinned.

"At the same time? Shut *up!*"

"Oh yes. I'm gonna be the center of attention for once. I'm having a ménage à trois."

"*No.*" Cindy tossed back the last of her amaretto and shuddered.

"Even if he hadn't been a complete ass, Jamison never could have given me what I need in the bedroom. No one man could."

Chapter Two

"This isn't such a good idea, Tatsu."

"Little brother, we have to get a date soon."

"But surely there's another way...?"

"Trust me. I don't need to remind you of the consequences if we ignore the signs much longer." He plopped on the side of his bed and took a long, fortifying swallow of his latte.

"No, you don't." Shrugging his shoulders to loosen his tight muscles, Yong sank back in the armchair and placed his cup on the table beside him.

"Besides, with an ordinary date, we'd be obligated to explain, but our one-night stand comes with no strings attached. She won't even know how to contact us afterward." *Not that she'll want to. She'll probably be so freaked out, she'll move to Ecuador to put more space between her and us.*

"So, how does it work?"

"Madame Eve arranged a match for the night, and then we can get back to normal."

"How did you find the service?" Yong was puzzled.

"Grandfather knew Eve from years ago. He assured me she is discreet and can be trusted with..." he glanced at the hotel room door before lowering his voice to continue, "...*anything*."

"Grandfather approved the plan then?"

"Yes, and we would do well to follow his advice. We're

running out of time."

Tatsu fidgeted with his cup before setting it on the bedside table.

"Is it uncomfortable?" Studying his older brother for any signs of the change, Yong cringed as Tatsu rubbed the drying skin on his forearm.

"It's nothing I can't handle."

"You better start using this." Yong tossed him a container.

"Thank you." Tatsu sighed, smoothing the Chinese herbal ointment over his withered skin.

"You're sure it's safe? I don't want anyone to get hurt, especially during—"

"We have a little time left, and with Eve's help, we should be fine."

"All right." Yong dropped his aching head into his palms. "We're messing with fire, though."

"If anything goes wrong, it'll happen to me first." Tatsu rubbed behind his left ear. "You know what to do."

"I know what to do, but it won't get that far."

෴

Yong ran to catch up with his brother as they raced through the crowded depot.

"Hurry!" Tatsu leapt onto the step as the train began to roll along the tracks.

Yong grabbed his hand and scrambled up beside him. "That was close," he said. "I'm so fed up with moving around." He plopped into a molded seat by the window, fighting down unease at the upcoming evening. Niagara falls—the honeymoon destination. *Ironic.*

"Let's just hope one night is enough to return everything to normal." Tatsu settled in beside him and tucked the worn leather journal inside his coat pocket.

"What if it's not?" Yong stared through the dirty window at the lampposts flying by at increasing speed while the train gained momentum.

"Listen, I promised I'd look after you, and I'll do what it takes to make sure at least *you* have a shot at a regular life, even if I don't make it."

"That won't happen. I couldn't survive without you, and I wouldn't want to."

"Don't say that." Tatsu grabbed his arm. "You deserve a chance at something wonderful, and I'm gonna make sure you have it. You just make sure you take it."

"You can't ask me to—" His throat grew thick.

"Hey, I won't debate the issue. Fate has chosen, and nature is running its course. Don't dishonor me by refusing." Tatsu pulled his coat sleeve down to his wrist, covering the drying skin. "You don't need to feel guilty. Everything happens as it's meant to."

"Grandfather said it doesn't have to."

"He said there is a chance it won't, a *small chance.*"

Yong swallowed hard, anger rising in his chest. "What makes me so special? Why is my life more important than yours? You deserve—" The gush of energy amplified into a shockwave of heat through the rest of his body.

"You have to calm yourself, now." A subtle fear filled Tatsu's eyes

"What's happening?" Yong gasped.

"Remember what Grandfather told us. The change is fueled by energy. You're getting angry; you have to relax." His brother's soothing tone helped.

"I've never felt like that before." Drawing in a deep breath, the tsunami receded, more so with every inhale.

"You've just had a taste of my side. What do you think?" The corners of Tatsu's mouth curled up and he settled back into his seat.

"It felt—" He couldn't find the words.

"Powerful?"

"*Yes.*"

Tatsu's weary eyes lit up a little, and then he drifted off to sleep. Paleness swept over his light brown skin and the dark hue of his full lips faded to grey. His square jaw line held the last of the strength in his face.

Sadness overtook Yong while he examined his identical twin. Born minutes earlier, he carried the wisdom of many generations. His role of protector was in danger. The energy transfer had drained him. Yong had to be more aware next time, more careful. He couldn't let that happen again.

Chapter Three

Cindy pulled up in the valet line of the Castillo Niagara Falls and turned off the truck. "Are you sure you don't want me to check into a room to be close by in case...?"

"Thanks, Cindy, but no. I'm a big girl." She flashed her friend a smile. "Madame Evangeline has an exemplary reputation; she ensures safety above all. I'll be okay. Besides, I can handle anything now."

But as she reached for the door handle, her courage failed. "Okay, let's park, out back. You can get a room." She shielded her face with her hand and turned away from the window. "Hurry up."

"Sudden change of heart?" Cindy stared. "You're crying. What's wrong? You don't want to go?"

Gwen pointed. A few feet away, her ex stood arm in arm with his soon-to-be-wife, while a porter loaded their luggage on a trolley.

"Jamison's here? Oh no." Cindy's voice cracked. She cranked the ignition but it wouldn't turn over. Clicking sounds replaced the confident purr of the engine.

"Cindy, please."

"Dammit, it won't start. Are you scared?"

"Of him or what I might do?"

"Both?"

"Terrified, hurry."

She turned the key again, pumping the gas. "Dammit, come on, come on." The clicking slowed, then died altogether. "For the love of—" Cindy smacked the steering wheel with her palm. The blare of the horn alerted the bystanders to their presence.

Mortified at the sight of her asshole ex glancing their way, Gwen dropped her head down between her knees, praying he hadn't identified her.

A knock on the glass startled her and she froze, not wanting to face her devastation.

"Gwen? Is that you?" His taunting chuckle ignited the rage she'd been suppressing for the last six months.

"Cindy," she straightened and glared toward her tormenter, "leave the truck. Let the valet deal with it—we're goin' in." She eyed the tramp standing behind Jamison, with her bony little arms folded across her chest. Gwen wanted to reach over and smack the sadistic smile off her surgically altered face. She shoved the door open with the force of her channeled fury, hitting him hard.

Clutching his bloodied nose, he let out a roar of pain. "What the hell did you do that for?"

"Jamison, I'm so sorry." She stepped out of the truck and slung her bag over her shoulder. "I suppose I didn't see you, standing there, *laughing at me*." Unable to hide her beaming triumph, she closed the door and headed for the hotel.

Jamison grabbed her arm and yanked her to him with a loud snarl, his eyes ablaze. "I oughta—"

A flash of terror rushed over her, but she refused to let it show.

"Hey." The doorman approached and Jamison let go, taking a step back.

"That's right, darling. I'm not yours to knock around anymore. And in case you've forgotten, I can take care of myself now." Gwen dropped her gaze to his scarred hand. With a cocky grin, she brushed past the doorman, heading for the entrance.

Cindy grabbed the suitcase from the trunk, and followed her.

"Jamison, geez." She tsked. "Now that's a shame. Katrina, you should get him seen by a doctor. You wouldn't want that nose bruised in the wedding pictures."

Gwen called over her shoulder. "Great to see you again, Ms. Harlot—I mean, Ms. Harlan. Good luck on your big day tomorrow, and after that. Lord knows, you're gonna need it."

"That was—" Cindy followed her into the lobby.

"Awesome. I haven't felt so good in years."

"After everything he's done to you, he got off easy."

જી

"I'm glad you let me stick around. You're gorgeous." Cindy fussed with Gwen's auburn tendrils, draping them down her back while she watched in the mirror.

"Thanks for being here and helping me get ready."

"Are you nervous?" She dabbed blush over Gwen's cheekbones.

"The butterflies in my stomach are doing jumping jacks, but I'm excited."

"Where are you meeting them?"

"Downstairs in the lounge." She grabbed her lipstick then moved over to the full-length mirror on the closet door to inspect her mocha bandage dress. Running her fingers along the crisscross block pattern, she winced. The outfit revealed more cleavage than she remembered seeing when she bought it.

"If you run into Jamison tonight, he'll bust a gut."

"Good. I hope it hurts."

"Stop fussing with your dress. It's perfect."

Gwen smoothed the maroon lipstick over her lips and paused, staring at her reflection.

"What is it?" Cindy came up beside her.

"Nothing, it's just that, it never occurred to me that I would ever sleep with another man. I thought I'd found the one." She held up her ring finger and studied the telltale strip of pale skin.

"You're gonna have a great time."

"Thanks, Cin. Hey, you could get a peek at them downstairs."

"I like that idea. Then I can spend the rest of my night romanticizing about your fantasy come true." Cindy pouted.

"Honey—"

"I'm fine, just envious."

"Do you want me to share tonight?" She chuckled. "After all, I have two."

"Of course not." Cindy grinned. "Let's get down there. I can't wait to see what they look like. Are you coming back here?"

"Madame Evangeline booked us into a guest house on the grounds. It's described as *secluded and unusual*."

"I suppose with all that bumping and grinding, you could use more privacy than accommodations in the main building would give."

"I imagine so." A twinge of anxiety settled in her stomach. "Anyway, I just realized that means you don't need to get another room. You can stay here. There's an incredible view of the falls out from the terrace." Gwen glanced over at the sheer curtain flowing in from the open glass door.

"How will you know who they are?"

"Madame Eve's message said they would have a champagne rose for me."

Chapter Four

*G*wen felt daring and ready. She took a seat at the bar, swinging her legs as she contemplated what to order.

She watched out of the corner of her eye as Cindy plopped into a leather armchair by the fireplace on the other side of the lounge. The deep mahogany and dark brown furnishings were accented by soft lighting and ambient jazz music playing, a perfect atmosphere for a discreet rendezvous.

"What can I get for you, miss?" A pretty blonde in a white shirt and apron stood behind the counter.

"I suppose a white wine spritzer?"

"Coming right up."

She scanned the room for two men with a rose, but only saw a few couples and, of course, Cindy. The crowd seemed sparse for cocktail hour. Returning her focus to her friend, Gwen saw her eyes widen.

What? She mouthed.

"Did you get all dolled up for me?" The heat of his breath on her shoulder made her recoil.

"Where is your bride-to-be?" She didn't turn around. Gwen looked back to Cindy's frightened stare, and casually held her palm up. She hoped to avoid a scene, but if it got bad, she'd use her backup.

"Here's your drink ma'am." The server pushed the wine glass

across the bar.

"Thank you." Pulling some cash from her purse, she laid it on the counter, ready to make her getaway.

Intrusive, as always, Jamison put one arm across the back of her chair and the other on the bar, speaking in the seductive tone she had grown to hate. "Katrina's busy for a while; can your husband buy you a drink?"

"Ex-husband, and no, you can't." Lifting her glass to sip, she hoped he'd take the hint, but he pulled up a stool beside her. "Have you forgotten about the restraining order?"

"That's just a piece of paper, love." Alcohol lingered on his breath when he spoke close to her ear. "Damn, you look good tonight, sweet enough to eat." He ogled her, making her stomach turn.

"You're drunk. Get away from me." She set her glass down and eased away from him.

"Come on, baby. For old times' sake?" He dropped a kiss on her shoulder while digging his fingers into her thigh with bruising force.

"Get your filthy paws off me, Jamison." She tried to shove his hand away.

"You're gonna play hard to get, huh?" His presumption sent a charge of anger through her, and she peeled his fingers off her leg. Laughing, he slid it up her back to her neck.

"I know you're here because of the wedding. You wanted one last chance to get me back. Maybe celebrate your birthday with a good round or two?" His arrogant words fueled her frustration, but she had no desire to lose control in a public place.

"Get your hands off me, or so help me...." Clenching her fists, she contained the simmering eruption.

"So help you what Gwen? Hmm, what are you gonna do?"

Gwen gasped when he tangled his fingers in the fine hairs at the base of her neck and tugged, his actions hidden by her long waves. She looked for the server, but she had stepped out to tend customers in the lounge.

Jamison's wrapped his other hand around her wrist, so tight

it felt as though he could snap it like a twig. He had become quite skilled at hiding his aggressive tendencies in public; he did have years of experience.

"Maybe we should go for a little walk." He stood, dragging her to her feet and using his fingers tangled in her hair to guide her toward the door.

Terrified, she looked to Cindy.

Help me? She mouthed. Her friend had stood up, but remained by her chair. A confused expression marring her features, she tugged at her foot; the heel of her shoe had caught in a groove in the hardwood floor.

He's going teach me a lesson for the car door incident. If I defend myself, I'll end up killing him this time. I can't react. Oh God, what do I do? But she had no choice—fists clenched; she prepared to free herself at all costs.

"Excuse me, Gwen?"

Jamison's grip loosened, but he kept his hand on her arm and his hold on her hair while he turned around with her.

"I'm sorry I'm late honey, I got caught up in traffic. What's going on here?" The dark haired stranger wore a fierce expression as he stepped closer to them and handed Gwen a champagne rose.

She accepted the bloom with relief. "Nothing at all. He's just leaving."

Jade green eyes glowed against his tanned complexion and black, shoulder-length hair, presenting an exotic, Asian appearance.

But Jamison hadn't let go yet. "Who the hell are you?"

"My date." She pried his fingers out of her hair, overwhelmed by the strangeness of the situation.

"Jamison, what are you doing down here? I've been searching everywhere for you." Katrina slouched in the doorway wrapped in a frumpy, long coat. With her arms folded over her chest and her disheveled locks of platinum hair pulled back into an unkempt bun, she looked like a train wreck. From her expression, she had deduced her fiancé's intentions in regard to his ex. He'd have a hard time talking himself out of the doghouse the night before their wedding.

Finally, Jamison released her wrist and her hair and stepped back. The mystery man held out his hand and Gwen accepted. He tugged her closer and slid his arm around her waist.

Encompassed by safety and drawn in by the tantalizing fragrance of spicy lavender and amber, she whispered, "Is that Drakkar I smell?"

"Yes, it is." He lifted his chin and tilted his head, inviting her to indulge. Enchanted, Gwen took in a long, savoring whiff.

With a final, confused glance over his shoulder, Jamison followed Katrina out, and Gwen's shoulders drooped in relief. Over by the fireplace, Cindy sat down and lifted her glass of wine with a quirky smile. Gwen focused again on her savior. "Thank you."

"Let's get you a drink." A smoldering grin lit his handsome face.

"You're—?" Forcing long breaths in and out, she tried to calm down.

"I'm Tatsu."

As knights in shining armor go...damn, he's hot.

He led her to a booth and sat her down. He obtained a baggie of ice from the barmaid and returned to apply it to her bruised wrist.

"Better now?"

Such kind eyes.

"Yes, thank you." She studied him with fascination, as he tended to her discomfort with a gentle touch.

"It doesn't seem broken, but maybe we should get it checked, just to be safe."

"I'm fine, it's not broken."

"How can you be sure?"

"I've had bro—" she caught herself in mid-disclosure, not wanting to reveal too much of her rocky past. "I'm okay. If it still hurts later, I'll get it treated."

"All right."

Gwen scanned the lounge. "Weren't there supposed to be two of you?"

"My brother will be here soon. He went to drop our things off at the guest house. Our train arrived late, and we didn't want to leave you waiting."

"Your brother?"

"Yes." He laughed.

"Hey, what did I miss?"

Am I seeing double? A second man slid into the curved booth on her other side.

"Hi, Gwen, I'm Yong."

"How do you do?" She held out her free hand.

He took it, pressing his lips to the back. "Very well, thank you." He focused on her bruised wrist, concern darkening his luminescent green eyes. "Is it broken?"

"We don't think so," Tatsu said.

"I'm all right, I just—" Embarrassment washed over her. It had been bad enough when one of them saw what happened, but to explain to the other?

"I know. It's okay, Gwen." Yong caressed her bare shoulder.

"You know?" Her eyes darted back and forth. When would Tatsu have had time to tell him? Yong's touch made logical thought difficult anyway.

"Being twins, we have sort of a link, a connection." Tatsu glared at him.

Gwen didn't understand what he meant, but she was fascinated by everything about the pair. "That's pretty amazing, like twin telepathy." She settled into the cushioned seat.

Tatsu and Yong spent the next hour drawing Gwen out, asking her about her life, her likes and dislikes—and her failed marriage. She answered in monosyllables, dazed by their smoldering eyes and the extreme warmth she experienced sitting between them.

"So, you were married to him for ten years?"

"Yong!" Tatsu scolded.

"What?"

"No, really, it's okay." She patted Tatsu's leather-clad arm, giving him a reassuring grin. "I don't mind sharing some history. A little intimacy tonight would be a good thing."

Tatsu nodded.

"In answer to your question, a very long ten years." She flexed her tender wrist under the table, trying not to remember the other injuries she'd sustained in that decade.

"How long have you been divorced?"

"I left him six months ago."

"He was a fool, letting you go." Tatsu took her left hand from his arm, held it in front of him, and stroked the back of it with gentle fingers.

"I can't argue with that." She giggled, ready to put the past behind her for the night.

"His loss is our good fortune, brother." Yong reached under the table, and collected her right hand, and pressed his lips to the backs of her fingers.

Desire swept through her.

"I—uh...." *How can I suggest we head back to the room without sounding overeager?*

"Gwen, would you care to join us at the guest house?"

"Tatsu, you must have been reading my mind," she replied, relieved and a bit puzzled. Had he read her mind? *Of course not!*

While Tatsu headed over to the bar to pay for their drinks, Yong stood at her side and extended his hand to help her to her feet.

"Thank you."

"My pleasure, my lady." He held her coat up while she slipped her arms into the sleeves, and then fastened the extra-large buttons with slow deliberation. Gwen wanted to step even closer to him; their gravitational pull was phenomenal.

"Okay, I think we're all set." Tatsu returned, and they headed through the lobby, each man holding one of Gwen's hands. Approaching the revolving doors, she paused, pulling the men to a stop. Katrina stood at the concierge desk next to a luggage rack piled with bulging suitcases, a bit of beaded white fabric protruding from the one on top.

"I don't care. I want my limo now."

"What is it?" Yong asked.

Katrina spun to face her. No amount of high-end foundation or eye makeup could conceal Jamison's handiwork. Memories came flooding back. Despite her dislike of the woman, Gwen couldn't see another of his victims suffer without someone to lend a hand. Without Cindy, she didn't know what she would have done.

"Excuse me for one minute, gentlemen." Gwen sighed and approached the trembling woman.

"Are you all right, Katrina?"

"Do I look all right?" The blonde's puffy cheeks and tear-swollen eyes belied her fierce tone.

"Where is he?"

"I don't know, and I don't care," she said, tipping her chin up. "Where is my God damn limo?"

A frustrated doorman clutched her arm. "But, Ms. Harlan, the police are on their way. You can't leave."

She shrugged him off. "The hell I can't."

"Look, Katrina." Gwen gripped her shoulders and gave her a gentle shake. "I understand exactly what you're feeling right now, but if you let him get away with it once, it's only going to get worse if you ever take him back. And I'm sure you know how persuasive Jamison can be."

"Since when do you care? I recall something along the lines of *good luck, you're gonna need it.* Sounds to me like you think I got what I deserved." Half shouting and half crying, she remained straight-backed and stiff-shouldered

"I'm really sorry I was such a smartass. No one deserves to be abused. Not you, not me...no one."

Tears began to stream down Katrina's cheeks. "I don't know what to do," she whimpered.

"Tell the cops everything. Don't try to protect him and *don't* take him back."

"The wedding—"

"—your life is more important."

Gwen sucked in a deep breath and took a step back. Slowly, she lifted her mass of curls to reveal the deep scar behind her right ear. "I've been hiding this since the night he did it to me."

Katrina stared.

"It could have been a lot worse tonight. Don't make the same mistake I did and let him do it more than once. It almost got me killed."

Gwen hugged her, wanting her to have some warmth on such an awful day. Katrina didn't respond, but that didn't matter.

"You'll survive. Sic your dad on him—or your brother. Do you have a brother?" At her nod, Gwen smiled. "And file that police report. I wish I had the first time." She offered a soft smile and walked away with a sense of relief, and in large part, forgiveness.

"Is everything okay?" Tatsu's concerned expression stood in stark contrast to what her past relationships had led her to expect from a man.

"Better now. Let's go."

Yong stopped short. "I almost forgot, the guest house room keycard wasn't working properly. I'd better have them check it while we're still here." He approached the concierge and Tatsu made to follow.

"Tatsu, while you deal with that, I'll just use the restroom, all right?" She pointed across the lobby.

"Sure, we'll meet you here." He lifted her hand and kissed her fingers. Her stomach fluttered at the warmth of his lips.

"Five minutes. I'll be right back."

Gwen followed the ladies room signs down the hallway, giddy with excitement. *Two men, all to myself? Their eyes, their handsome faces, I can't wait to see what's under their leather jackets.*

As she pushed on the door, she was dragged backward by a large hand around her chest. Another clamped over her mouth. Kicking and flailing, she clutched at the fingers, trying to pry them away.

"Shut up." *Shit.* She knew that voice.

Jamison dragged her out the door at the end of the hall. The heels of her stiletto boots scraped across the threshold and onto the hardness of the snow-covered ground as she kicked.

"Stop fighting bitch." His grip tightened; the vicious force against her ribcage grew as his fingertips burrowed deep into her side. The familiar sour odor of his breath filled her nose as he pressed his stubbly cheek against hers.

He shoved her away and she landed on her side with a painful thud. The sharpness of the crystallized snow dug into her hips and thighs. She scrambled to her feet. "Jamison, what the hell is your problem?" A spark ignited inside her, the rising heat overtaking her pain.

"Did you think I was gonna forget the car door?" He grabbed a handful of her hair, yanking her back to face him. She teetered, trying to balance as her heels sank into the slippery snow.

She grabbed his fist and pushed down on his knuckles, ducking down and pulling free. He grabbed her by the throat and she stomped on his foot with her spiked heel and shot her fists up between his elbows and out. She stumbled back, the palms of her hands burning hot. Buzzing filled her ears. Sound faded, and her vision became a wash of red.

"You bitch." He hobbled.

"You inspired me to take self-defense classes. You're never gonna lay a hand on me again." A powerful explosion of energy flowed through her. Flames filled her throat and she was no longer in control. Her worst fears unfolded before her horrified eyes.

"Gwen, it's okay, it's me Tatsu." Barely audible, his words coaxed her back to awareness of her surroundings.

"Hey, look at me, please?" He cupped her cheeks, his palms cool on her hot skin.

"That's it, look at me. I'm right here."

Chapter Five

*H*er high body temperature told Tatsu what was happening. He felt it himself in times of fury. *A moment later, and she would have burned the bastard to a crisp. Maybe not a bad thing…. No, we'd never be able to explain the charred corpse.*

"Gwen, focus on me." He patted her face, working to rouse her from her trance. Her eyes glowed orange.

Yong, keep him away, I've got this.

Whatever you're gonna do, do it fast. Yong's thoughts held panic. Tatsu could feel the frenzy set in, and the acute stinging of his shoulder blades took hold, his flesh beginning to tear.

To his left, Yong restrained the belligerent drunk face-down in the snow; he wouldn't be able to witness anything. Yong's body was rising in heat too; flooding with adrenaline, it was fueling their change.

This wasn't how he'd wanted their first kiss to be, but he considered it a necessary sacrifice. Insatiable desire rushed through him when he claimed her delectable lips. At first, she hesitated then accepted his touch.

He pulled back for a moment. "That's it, sweetie, let it go, I've got you. Everything's going to be okay." He captured her mouth again. The consuming heat didn't faze him in the least. He welcomed it. The sweetness of her fevered tongue intoxicated him. "Yes, that's it, give it to me, I can handle it." Tatsu sucked in her flaming breath, absorbing the energy, drawing out the last of her ferocity. She brought her hands up, placing them over his, holding them tight.

"It's all right now; you're fine." Tatsu kissed her forehead; her flesh had cooled and her chocolate brown eye color had returned.

Yong, take her back to the guest house. I'll handle him; we can't afford for you to lose control now.

What about you?

I'll be fine. I'll just finish up with our friend.

Yong jumped up, leaving Jamison slumped in the snow. He flung off his bomber jacket, wrapped it around Gwen's shaking shoulders, over her own, lighter coat, and scooped her up into his arms. She hung motionless with a fixed stare.

She's in shock. Take care of her. I'll be right there.

Tatsu eyed the beast clambering to his feet in front of him, as his brother disappeared toward the guest house.

"You might want to think, before you try anything stupid." The internal flames were consuming him, and he doubted his ability to stay his hand should the fool continue to threaten their woman.

When Jamison lunged forward with a bellow, Tatsu gathered the last of his self-control and stepped aside. The angry man flew face first to the ground.

"Stay down or you'll leave me no choice."

"Fuck you," Jamison growled, pulled himself upright, and charged again.

"Okay, that's it." Tatsu caught him by the throat and squeezed hard. His opponent dropped to his knees, gasping. "Stay away from Gwen."

"What's with your eyes? They're glowing."

Tatsu sent him crashing backward to the ground. "Next time I won't be so nice."

He spied a row of enormous icicles hanging from the edge of the rooftop over Jamison.

"You can't protect her forever. I'll find her, and when I do...."

Tatsu plotted his target along the eaves trough and opened

his mouth, hurling flames at the daggers of ice.

"What the fuck?" Frozen spears pierced the ground around him, and Jamison curled into a ball, arms wrapped around his head.

Tatsu released the flame and his body temperature shot back down to normal. Agony surged through his shoulder blades.

"Gwen is off limits to you." He maintained his stare until the other man nodded in agreement.

Grateful no hotel guests had wandered out during their melee, Tatsu trudged away from Jamison. He smoothed back his hair and straightened his coat. As he reached the front of the hotel, a police car screeched to a halt and a pair of officers spilled out. The driver ducked his head to the side, speaking into his shoulder radio.

"Dispatch, be advised, we are on scene and searching for the suspect."

"Hey, officers, I think the person you're looking for ran back there. Be careful of falling ice though, looks dangerous." Buttoning his jacket, Tatsu crossed the bridge, heading toward the guest house and the most important evening of his—and his brother's—life.

☙

Yong sat on the couch with Gwen, his arm protectively around her, when Tatsu came in and shut the door, shoulders slumped.

"Wow, this is different, a tunnel for a room?" Tatsu glanced around at the arch shaped walls.

"Unique, isn't it?" She smiled. "Look at the window at the end. It's like peering out from inside a globe. You can see the water falling."

"It's beautiful."

"Are you okay?" Yong asked.

"I'm fine. How are you, Gwen?"

"Better, thanks to you both."

35

She nuzzled into his embrace, and Yong snuggled her close.

Concerned, he sent a quick thought. *I felt your fire. Did he see anything?*

Nothing anyone would believe.

What is it? Yong stood, sensing his brother's pain.

"Okay, what's going on here?" She went to Tatsu, patting him down. "Did Jamison hurt you?"

"It's all right, nothing to worry about." He turned away from her with a grimace. "The police arrived, so they were dealing with him. He smelled like a fifth of rye, probably headed for the drunk tank to sleep it off."

"Thank God," she sighed.

Tatsu, it's started, hasn't it?

Don't scare her, please. Maybe we should send her back to the hotel.

No, she can handle it, I think. Let's give her a chance.

"Hey you two, knock it off with the twin mind-reading already. Talk to me."

"It's a long story. Not what you signed up for tonight." Tatsu brushed past them and sat down on the black suede couch.

"In case you forgot, neither of you signed up for dealing with my psycho ex, either."

"True, but this goes beyond—"

"Let's get down to the nitty gritty. What are you two? Shape shifters or something?"

"What?" Double sounds of shock filled the air.

"I read, you know...all kinds of science fiction and paranormal. There is no way you could be human, not with how you managed me just now. Yong told me everything. I could have burned him alive, and you took over like you deal with this weird shit all the time."

"Gwen," Yong pleaded.

"We're in this situation together, so I need to know who I'm involved with...or what?" Hands on hips, she tapped the toe of her stiletto boot on the floor. "Do you think I would or *could* tell anyone about you after what happened to me tonight? I'm not so normal myself these days."

Yong stared at Tatsu. *I don't know what to say to her.*

She's our last chance; it's now or never. "We are human," Tatsu said.

Yong sat beside him and leaned back.

"You are?"

"Half, anyway."

"Half human? What about the rest of you?" Her widened eyes darted between them.

Yong pulled a brown leather journal from his coat pocket and handed it to her.

She flipped through the pages. "I can't read it."

"It's written in kanji—Chinese calligraphy."

"I can see that much. What's it about?"

Yong patted the couch between them. He took the book as she snuggled in. "Our grandfather started his journal as a boy and kept writing over the decades, knowing he would have to pass the information down someday."

"About what?"

"Chinese culture sometimes refers to our people as "Descendants of the Dragon.""

"Go on."

"We're parahuman—half-breeds."

Gwen shrank back, staring blankly at the page.

We're going about this all wrong, little brother.

Gimme a minute.

"Our mother didn't hook up with a dragon, or anything bizarre like that, but we believe we evolved from them centuries ago. Grandfather's research says that our people carry the dormant gene, and twins born during the year of the dragon receive the dominant version."

"I'm listening."

"We were born in 1976, the year of the dragon."

"So what does that mean?"

"Legend has it, twins born under that Chinese zodiac sign are in fact one dragon's spirit, split in two."

"So we're talking talons and scales, with wings and fiery breath?"

"Not yet, but it could happen. The tales say one twin will at some point overpower the other. The stronger one will remain human. The other will shift into the form of a dragon then die—reuniting the spirit in one body."

"So, you believe the story? The ramblings of your grandfather's lifelong obsession with legends?"

"Of course we do."

"Why? It's just fiction. People write about that kind of stuff all the time."

"Fiction is often based on some element of truth. Grandfather was born in 1940."

"What's your point?"

"The year of the dragon."

"And?"

"He's the surviving twin."

She got to her feet and looked from Yong to his brother. "Stand up, right now."

The brothers complied. She circled them at a slow pace.

"Take your coats off."

Tatsu shook his head.

"Please." She stepped in front of him and cupped his pale cheek in her palm. He allowed his leather coat to drop to the floor.

Running her hands along both their chests, she frowned. "Now your shirts."

Tatsu winced, sucking in a breath as he lifted the turtleneck sweater over his head.

"What are these tattoos on your chests? They're the same." Her fingers glided over the markings.

"The kanji symbol means double dragon," Tatsu said.

"Twin dragons?"

He gave a soft smile. "Yes."

She stepped behind Yong, and continued her gentle exploration with her nails along his bare back. Next, she moved behind Tatsu and clapped her hand over her mouth.

"Does it hurt?" Her eyes welled up.

Yong feared what he would find. "No, it can't be." Approaching, he swallowed hard at the sight of the jagged flesh and touched the nubs of wings poking out of Tatsu's back.

"How can we stop it?" Her voice was frantic.

"I'm not sure we can anymore." Tatsu said.

"We could have before? How?"

"It doesn't matter now. We shouldn't have gotten you involved."

"The book states," Yong tried to keep defeat from overwhelming him, "the way to keep the change from happening is to cancel the exchange of energy flow between us, basically short circuiting it."

"Grandfather had a theory," Tatsu said.

"What was it?"

"If both of us were to—experience the identical explosive force at the same time, it would neutralize the event and put a stop to it, for good." Yong met her narrow-eyed probing stare.

"I'm not following you."

"Think about it for a minute. What is the one thing all humans consider the ultimate mind-blowing experience?" He took her hands in his.

"You mean like when I raged before?"

"No, angry energy feeds the change. We couldn't both lose control like that at the same time. One of us is always less reactive, so one will still overpower the other." Tatsu said.

"Anger is the highest peak I can think of. What else is there?" Yong responded, mindful not to frighten her. "Orgasm."

"What?" Her head snapped back, and she pulled her hands away. "Oh, *oh*." Her heart-shaped face turned bright red.

"I know how it sounds, but that's why Grandfather had Madame Eve set us up for a ménage. The best chance to have the same frenzied shockwave would be to—climax at the same time. We just didn't expect the change so soon."

She took a step back, frowning. "Couldn't you have solved

your problem, a long time ago by—pleasing yourselves at the same time?"

"It's different." Tatsu returned to the couch. "There's a much greater response during sex with partners than during masturbation. It's the connection between the mates, a package deal. Maybe it's a dragon thing, but the mental, emotional, and physical turn on at the same time is the ultimate. You know what I mean?"

"That, yes, I do understand, but climaxing at the same time, that could be tricky to achieve."

"Very." Tatsu's voice was filled with doubt.

"Why is all of this happening now?"

"Over the past several years, if one of us got riled up over something, it created—a quickening. Each time, it became more potent, until the energy started to shift. Tatsu has always been the more hot-headed twin, so he became stronger, but recently, something changed, and I started absorbing him instead."

"If you thought it would take longer, why is it happening so fast?" Gwen drew closer again, looking into his eyes with fascination.

"We think, because it's 2012, another year of the dragon. The last surge we experienced was in 2000—it's the only thing that makes sense."

"Why couldn't you have cured it when you had sex before? Either of you?"

"Uh—that." Yong covered his mouth with his hand through a fake cough.

"What?"

He winced at Tatsu's hanging head and went over to the mini bar behind them, pulling out a bottle of cognac and three glasses, splashing generous amounts for each of them.

"Here, you're gonna need a drink." He handed one glass to Gwen and another to his brother.

"You're scaring me." Her shapely lips distracted him, and her cleavage didn't help his focus any.

"The truth is, I've never been with a woman before." He

chugged back his drink.

"You're gay?" Her mouth fell open.

"What? No, I'm not gay. I'm a—a—"

"Yong, are you a virgin?"

"Yes." He turned back to the bar and grabbed the bottle, serving up another glass of courage.

"What about you?" She looked over at the wincing man on the couch.

"Uh—yeah, same here."

"Sweet Jesus, are you guys kidding me?"

Yong placed his fingers under her glass and tipped it up. She swallowed the contents and choked out, "Virgins?"

"Look, it's okay if it's too much for you. I half expected you to bolt when you saw my back," Tatsu said.

"No, it's not that at all—this is a lot of pressure for a one-night stand. I'm no expert in bed."

Silence filled the tunnel-shaped apartment. Gwen shook her head. Yong was sure she was contemplating the mess they'd put her in. Guilt permeated his mind and he walked over to the wall-sized window to watch the crashing falls through the dome-shaped glass.

"Gwen?" Tatsu said.

"Yes?"

"I know you handle fire like a dragon, but how did you get the ability?"

Returning to the couch, Yong nodded. "Good question."

"I don't know. It had never happened to me before until the night—"

"What night?"

Letting out a big sigh, she dropped down between them. "The night I almost died, about six months ago."

"What happened?" Tatsu asked, taking her hand.

"I found out my ex was cheating on me with his accounting client, and told him I knew."

"And then what?"

"I've never lost complete control like that before, I was raised to keep things to myself, not to complain, so most of the time I tolerated him."

"Go on." Yong urged her.

"What happened?" Tatsu gripped her hand.

"He had one of his violent spells, and I woke up in a pool of my own blood."

Yong caressed her back, encouraging her to tell as much as she felt comfortable with.

"All I can remember about that night is that everything went dark red, and then I blacked out. I woke up in the hospital. My friend Cindy had stopped by and...well, she called 911."

"You had a concussion?"

"Yes. Later, when we were alone, Cindy told me what she saw when she arrived."

"What?"

"She saw him holding me by the throat, and I grabbed his hand and burned him—with my fingers."

"What's your heritage?" Tatsu watched her with an intense glare.

"I'm not sure. I'm adopted. I only know I'm of mixed race."

"What about your birth family?"

"My adoptive parents told me my birth mother couldn't keep me. She was young and single. They didn't know anything about my father. They did tell me one other thing."

"What was that?"

"Well, they said she had been pregnant with twins, but lost one before birth."

"Wait a minute, Gwen. What year were you born?"

"'76."

"The same year we were born?" Yong whispered with wide eyes.

Tatsu stood up and paced back and forth.

"Do you realize what you're saying?"

"Wow, it didn't occur to me earlier, but, yes, I think I do."

"She's a dragon." Both men declared.

"Un-friggin'-believable." He shook his head. "Grandfather

42

said Madame Eve would find the perfect match—you don't think she knew?"

"What, that I could be—no, it's impossible."

"Yet, here we are, with the perfect mate for us. We couldn't have planned it better; you can handle the heat and the risk of flames. She *is* the one."

"That is, if you even want to consider—" Yong met her stunned gaze and put his arm around her. "Are you all right?"

"I think I'm better than that."

"Really?"

"Yeah, I just assumed it was because I was adopted, but I've never fit in anywhere, and since that horrible night, I thought something was *seriously* wrong with me."

"Do you still want to?" Tatsu kneeled in front of her, the corners of his mouth curled back.

"Do I want to bust your cherries?" She blushed.

"Um—yeah, that."

Chapter Six

*T*atsu kissed the back of her fingers with a long, slow sweetness that made her toes curl. Yong inched closer, smoothing her hair back, placing tender kisses along her shoulders and up her neck.

The slightest contact of their lips to her skin was intoxicating.

"There is something to be said for your enthusiasm, gentlemen."

"It seems you'll be our teacher this evening." Still kneeling in front of her, Tatsu glided his hands over her boots and along the outsides of her thighs.

"So I guess I should teach you guys a little *tongue-fu?* Since we're working at beginner's level, that is." Her giggles were short-lived when the boys stood up, tugging her to her feet with tantalizing smiles.

"Where should we start?" Tatsu whispered in her ear then captured her lobe with heated lips. Finding it difficult to focus with his attentions and the distraction of Yong continuing to worship the other side, devouring her neck, Gwen tilted her head back. They were driving her wild with their mouths running along her flesh.

"I'm curious, gentlemen."

"What is it?" Tatsu asked between sucks on her neck.

"How is it neither of you have ever been with women before?"

"We were worried it would be too dangerous." Tatsu

squeezed her breast with gentle fingers.

"And now, with me?"

"You aren't just any woman." Yong ran his fingers along the small of her back. "You are *the* woman. You're a dragoness."

Liking his reply, Gwen was eager to get down to business. "Yong, undo my dress." Facing her other object of desire, her excitement grew as he complied, easing open the clasp. Sliding the form-fitting garment down her shoulders and over her hips, he dropped it to the floor. Gwen's sensitive peaks pushed hard against the confines of her lace bra.

"Tatsu, would you—?" She nodded at her leather boots.

"It would be my honor." He unzipped one knee-high boot and eased it off, and then the other, finishing by massaging her foot.

"Let's take you to the bed, shall we?" Yong took her hand and led the way, with Tatsu right behind.

Her magnificent twins eased her back onto the red jacquard silk bedspread and stood at her command.

"There are candles on the end tables—?"

"As you wish." Yong trailed his hand down her foot, and she shuddered.

Gwen watched with amazement as her double dragons went from candle to candle and blew on the wicks, igniting them. In moments, they had the room illuminated with the glow of red pillars and flickering flames. The heavenly scents of jasmine and roses swathed her.

When they returned to the bedside, she sat up. "Take off your pants."

Both pairs of jeans fell to the floor, leaving her with a splendid eyeful of something she grew impatient for.

"Identical in every department, I see." Inching forward on the mattress, she inspected the leanness of their abs with her fingertips, and stroked down to their dicks. Wrapping their cocks in her hands, she gave slow, pressured strokes up and down.

The sight of them rolling their heads back with eyes closed was empowering.

"Time to play." Taking the head of Tatsu's cock into her

mouth, she teased with her flicking tongue and then licked around the rim, evoking a low groan from him. At the same time, she continued to palm Yong's shaft, squeezing and releasing, smearing the bit of precum around with a fingertip.

The delectable sensation of her tongue cradling his swelling cock spurred her on. His dick hardened with each dip of her head, making it difficult to pace herself.

Sliding his fingers through her hair and holding on, he pulled her closer, easing deeper into her mouth, and she sucked harder. His hips and his breathing quickened. She pulled away.

"It's your first time; I don't want you to come too fast. I'm afraid it might not work." Stroking him again, she moved to Yong's rigid flesh and lapped at his head then worked his cock slowly in and out of her mouth.

Retreating, she smiled up at him. "Same goes for you, my dear; we can't have you losing control too soon."

Lying back on the bed, she allowed them to remove her remaining garments. Her nipples hardened in the cool air.

As their mouths moved up her shins, and across the inside of her knees, she wiggled with delight. Tatsu crept up to lie next to her and rested on one elbow, captivating her with his smoldering jade green eyes. Yong remained between her legs, exploring every inch of her skin with tongue and teeth.

Tatsu descended upon her lips and delivered an all-consuming kiss. Their tongues danced and curled.

"I want to taste you." Yong's ravenous mouth traveled along the inside of her thigh, sucking and nibbling on the sensitive skin at her bikini line. Spreading her legs wider, he gathered her juices on a fingertip and circled her clit. When she moaned, he chuckled and pulled away, leaning in to blow against her oversensitive tissues.

Starving for more of Yong's feeding frenzy, she reached for him, whimpering. Her desperation mounted, wanting more of each of them. Gwen rubbed her clit, inviting Yong to sample her moisture.

One dragon lingered with breathtaking kisses, the other

glided his tongue along the outer folds of her pussy. He paused for a moment, and Gwen glanced down. He grinned and buried his face in her mound.

"That's it, right there. Oh, that feels amazing." She rolled her hips in little circles, struck by an idea. "Tatsu, I want you to suck my clit. Yong, come here."

Yong assumed his brother's position and gave her a long, feathery, slow, building kiss that drew her in.

Tatsu skipped past the subtlety phase and captured her clit between his teeth.

"Oh, you're driving me crazy," she panted, between kisses. As a rolling wave of white hot spasms shot through her core, he lapped up her juices. He drove his finger deep inside her, and she whimpered at every flick, every lick of his tongue at her tender, swollen clit. Gwen forced herself still, wanting to experience every sensation of this remarkable moment.

"I can't take much more." She eased Yong back and lifted up on her elbows. "Tatsu, do you have any condoms and lube?"

She caught his unmistakable smirk. "Now? You're ready?"

"I'm more than ready—it's time to wrap the dragons."

Before she could blink, the multi-pleasure pack landed on the bed and a bottle of liquid rolled beside it.

"Are you sure you two are virgins?" Shaking off the residual tremors, she sat up and grabbed the package, tearing it open with shaky fingers.

"Well, we have—tried before, but never got this far." Tatsu's sheepish look made her pause.

"What is that supposed to mean?"

"A few years ago, we had a double date, hoping to cure our problem." Yong sat up.

"What happened?"

"We sort of, got overexcited, and—" Tatsu turned away, covering a muffled laugh.

"And?"

"His date left sort of quickly." Yong said, grinning. "We had to call it a night."

"Why did she leave?" Puzzled, she glanced between the brothers. "What's so funny?"

"Tracey—needed to—tend to her hair."

"I don't get it?"

"What Tatsu is trying to avoid saying is he got so aroused, he breathed fire—lying on top of her—ready to—"

"I get the picture, then what?"

"I messed up her hair." Tatsu shrugged, looking like the cat that swallowed the canary.

"He set it on fire."

"*What?*"

"I didn't realize hair spray could be so flammable."

"You're not wearing much hair spray, are you?"

"Excuse me?" She patted down her tousled mane.

"He's kidding, Gwen."

"Oh my God, you two are awful!" She slapped at their bare, solid chests, embarrassed at falling for the joke.

"Let me make it up to you, princess." Tatsu captured her lips with a deep, sensual kiss.

Gwen closed her eyes, savoring the flavor of his tongue and pulled back, wanting another glimpse of his brilliant green eyes. She grabbed a plastic wrapper and tore the corner with her teeth.

"Who's first?"

"Without triggering the shift of life force—we're not sure how—" Yong's brows furrowed and his chin dropped to his chest,

"Hey, I'm pretty sure your grandfather's book was more specific than that. Wasn't it his idea for the ménage?" She held up the second condom.

"Are you sure?"

"We'll work through it, Tatsu." She trailed her fingers over his lips and down the steely contours of his chest. "But, we need to infuse some logic here, too." She tried to peek at the almost forgotten deformity.

"The change began with you, so we have to make sure you get a boost first." She took out the rubber ring and rolled it onto his cock.

"Would it hurt you to lie on your back?" She caressed his broad shoulders.

"I think I can manage." One corner of his mouth pulled back into a smirk, bringing her some relief from the sense of doom that lingered about them. She traced the outline of his handsome face, and gave a slow, deep, searching kiss, trying to push aside her fear of what could become of one of her dragons.

Tatsu lay in the middle of the king-sized bed, wrapped and ready for her to redeem him.

"Yong," She tore the second package open and sheathed his cock, working to sound confident. "Are you okay with—taking the other side?"

"Other—oh—you want me in your..." His face filled with flushing redness.

"Would you mind fucking me in the ass?"

"You need me to answer that?" He chuckled. "I don't want to hurt you, though."

"We'll go slow. Keep the lube close by." She leaned in and claimed him with a provocative kiss then pulled away. "I've never had sex be a life or death matter, I sure hope you picked the right girl."

"Lady, and yes, we did. Regardless of the outcome, Gwen, I'm glad we connected. You're a remarkable woman." Tatsu gripped her bare hips as she straddled him. A tear collected at the rim of her eye; she was determined not to let him see it.

"This has to work." In a slow, rhythmic manner, she slid back and forth over his cock, grazing her clit, feeling the excessive heat seeping from his pelvis. Closing her eyes, she collected her hope and reached between her legs. She watched his expression when she eased herself onto the thickness of his head then slid over his shaft.

"Oh." The splendid heat filled her pussy, and she moved up and down on the rock hard flesh, sinking lower each time.

Consumed with the mind-blowing sensation of him inside her, she dragged his fingers up to her breasts. The length of his cock filled her with sweet agony, the pleasure multiplied as he squeezed and pinched her nipples.

"Ah—"

Gwen looked over her shoulder to find Yong trying to reach behind him, his face a mask of pain.

"It's starting isn't it? The energy?"

"Yes," Yong doubled over.

Stopping in mid thrust, she held Tatsu deep inside her. She fought the desperate urge to move.

"The lube, bring it here."

Yong trickled the cool fluid down her lower back, drizzling it over her ass.

"That's it, now spread it around and get me ready for you." She guided his hand, distributing the slippery fluid across her skin and over his intended target.

"I want you to begin with your finger. Ease it in with the lube, then insert two."

"Got it," he huffed.

"Are you all right?"

"Fine." Gentle, but persistent, he followed her directions.

She gasped at the sharp penetration of his finger sliding into her ass.

"Gwen?"

"It's okay, don't stop. I've never done this before, but I'll be fine. Keep going."

Sheer delight washed over her at the double penetration. She wanted more.

"Yong, two fingers. I can't hold back. Give it to me, please." She tilted her pelvis on Tatsu's cock, and rolled her hips, bringing on erotic pleasure. Two fingers increased to three, and the sensation became liberating.

"More lube. I want you inside of me, now."

The drizzle of wetness down her ass aroused her more. "Take me now."

His hard fingers retreated to be replaced with the tip of his cock.

"That's it; ease it in, a little at a time." All of a sudden, she felt like an expert calling all the shots.

Yong sank into her, filling her with a stinging, sweet sensation.

"Oh God, that's it." She panted and moved again on Tatsu's shaft.

Riding what soon became a rhythmic beat, she reveled in the explosive feeling of both dragons plunging inside her, then retreating. She arched in ecstasy.

"I'm gonna explode," she cried. "Tatsu?"

"I'm okay, don't stop, babe. Keep going." He winced, digging his fingertips into her hips.

"Yong?" She tried to look over her shoulder.

"Good, I'm good." Yong gasped, driving into her faster. "Gwen, God, you're so tight. I can't hold on. I'm gonna come."

"Tatsu, are you close?"

"Yes."

"Yong, deeper." She reached behind her, scratching at his hips, wanting him closer to her, seeking that piercing bliss as he buried his cock even farther than before.

"Tatsu, rub my clit," she begged, guiding his hand over her swollen pussy. He flicked and rubbed her tender nub.

"Oh yeah, that's it, oh—oh—" she shrieked. Her thighs tightened, her back stiffened, and her vaginal muscles clenched around Tatsu's cock.

"I feel you coming Gwen." Tatsu's breathing sped up.

Yong plunged into her with powerful thrusts. "Oh, I'm—I'm—uh..." He pulled her hips, hammering her ass, and convulsed. Slowing his pace, he pushed deep and hard.

"Holy fuck, Gwen, oh—oh," Yong rested against her back, shaking.

"Uh." Tatsu wailed.

Gwen looked down slowing her rhythm, and took in a sharp breath. A stabbing pain shot through her hips. "*No*, Tatsu." She collapsed on his chest.

"I'm sorry," He pulled his hands back, his fingernails morphed into claws, his right arm covered with dark green scales.

"Yong, help me!" she screamed.

He pulled out and scrambled to her side. "It didn't work. It's my fault."

"It's not too late. Yong, help me."

"What do I do?"

"Get something to tie his hands down, or he'll rip me to shreds." Yong disappeared from her line of vision before she finished speaking.

Tatsu's ragged breathing grew heavier, and his voice shifted into a fierce snarl. His jade eyes had transformed into glowing, red slits with almond shaped pupils.

"Yong, you know what to do. You promised," he bellowed. "Behind my ear. Do it now."

"What are you talking about?" She stared at him in disbelief. "This isn't happening. Hold on Tatsu, please."

"Yong knows what to do. Get away, Gwen. It's too dangerous. I don't want to hurt you."

"Hurry, Yong." Tatsu's cock felt as though it was growing bigger inside her. She held his hands above his head and moved in long strokes, up and down.

"It's okay. It's gonna work. I know it."

Tatsu began to convulse, he arched, roaring. She wasn't prepared for what came next. She screamed.

"What is it?" Yong returned with strips of shredded material from the bathroom shower curtain.

"Look," she pointed at his shoulders. Tatsu's back deformity had mutated into fully formed wings, expanding out to the sides.

"Yong, behind my ear, now."

"What's he talking about?"

"There's a kill spot, behind his left ear. He made me promise to kill him if the change happened." Tears flooded down Yong's cheeks. "I can't, brother, I can't."

"You won't need to. Tie his hands to the bedposts. Tie them strong."

Yong sprang into action, doing as she said.

"Now his feet." She began shifting up and down again,

bursting inside from the pressure of his cock.

"Uh—" Tatsu grunted.

"That's it, come for me. Come inside me. I'm yours." She trailed her hands down his chest; his skin had dried and begun to flake. "Let go baby, please." She drove onto him.

His body temperature, now scorching hot, melted the silk bedspread. The blazing heat didn't faze her at all.

"Yong, get back," she warned. Tatsu's breath blew searing heat over her naked body. "You're close, Tatsu; I can feel you pulsing inside me. It's time."

He thrashed beneath her; she writhed with burning. His body stiffened and he let out a thunderous roar.

"Yes, Tatsu, that's it, my dragon." She slowed her pace as he released with violent spasms.

"Ah, yes."

"Gwen, nothing's changed, he's still—" Yong moved closer, inspecting his features. "It didn't work."

Tatsu's breath grew shallow and deathly calm washed over his mangled body. His fiery eyes fluttered, and then closed.

"Tatsu? Don't you dare, don't give up." She broke into sobs and ran her trembling hands up to his sallow face. "You can't, not now."

Watching him lie there, motionless, a wave of scalding heat rushed through her.

"Gwen, what's happening to you? What are you doing?" Yong gripped her arm, and then bellowed in pain.

Barely able to hear or see him, consuming red overtook her vision, and sound faded away. All she could see were tantalizing lips, calling to her inner animal. She leaned down and delivered a soft kiss to her motionless dragon. Tenderness swept over her and the intensity of her yearning for him magnified.

"Tatsu, come back to me." She lingered against his cooling mouth. Her head ached. Her stomach flared with stabbing pain, and then everything faded to black.

જી

"Gwen?" The sound of his voice grew closer, as she tried to lift her pounding head. "Sweetie, wake up, please?"

She collected her senses and forced her heavy lids open.

"What happened, Yong?" She searched her memory. "Oh my God, Tatsu?"

"I'm right here."

She focused and saw her double dragon.

"It worked?" She sat up in bed, wrinkling her nose at the scent of the charred bedding underneath her.

"Yes, it did. It was you all along." Tatsu caressed her face with his palm.

"What do you mean?" She was still naked, but for the comforting warmth of Yong's bomber jacket draped over her.

"Don't you remember what you did?" Yong took her hand.

"What happened to you, Yong?" She inspected the wrapped gauze.

"A minor casualty, in the midst of everything." He gave a wink. "You don't remember?"

"No."

"Tatsu almost died. You saved his life."

"How?" She looked at their jade green eyes with relief.

"You breathed fire into me." Tatsu said. "You gave me your energy."

"I did?"

"According to Grandfather, that's a dragon's bond—the mating bond."

"Your grandfather?"

"We called him; we weren't sure what to do."

"How long have I been out?"

"A few hours; your temperature is back to normal, now."

"It wasn't before?"

"No, you were running a bit of a fever." Yong chuckled.

"How high?"

"We—couldn't figure that out."

"Oh?"

"Yong went to the hotel and grabbed some first aid stuff and a thermometer." Tatsu smoothed his hand over her bandaged hips.

"Oh, yeah, and...?"

"Before we could get a reading, you melted the thermometer." They smiled at her. "Our dragoness." Yong gave her a sexy grin.

"What about you?" She reached for Tatsu, turning him to the side, examining his bare back.

She observed bandages, but nothing unusual.

"You're normal now?"

"Well, almost." Yong kissed her hand and got up.

"You're still the same?" She looked back and forth.

"We're better than that. We're both safe now. Thanks to you, it's over."

"I can't believe it worked." She threw her arms around Tatsu and squeezed him tight.

"There's only one problem now."

"What's that, Yong?"

"We're kinda hooked on you; do you think you could handle two dragons around for a little while?"

Watching them both, she eased back into the pillow.

"What?" Tatsu's brows furrowed.

"I get two of you to myself?"

"We can see how it plays out, if you like."

"That all depends."

"On what?"

"How's my hair? Did you singe it?"

They burst out into laughter.

"Oh, one more thing." Tatsu patted her hand.

"Yes?"

He nodded at the bar behind him.

"Got it." Yong got up, walked over to the bar, and grabbed something from the counter. He backed toward her, hiding it in front of him.

"What's going on?"

"It's after twelve."

"Okay, so?"

"Happy birthday," they recited. Yong turned around with an elegant, white-iced cake.

"How did you know?"

"Madame Eve arranged to have the cake left in the bar fridge, with a note, we were to say happy birthday after midnight."

"That's so sweet," she gushed, reaching for it.

"Oh, hold on, we're missing something."

"Right here." Yong held up two candles, and stood beside Tatsu, handing him one. They blew on the wicks, igniting them.

"Make a wish."

"It already came true." Gwen blew out the candles and took the cake, placing it on the end table. She removed the jacket and lay back on the bed, ready for her gift.

DAMNATION & DESIRE

BY

KALI WILLOWS

Chapter One

*F*lipping through the pages of the crumbling Latin text with growing disturbance, Tessa felt the thumping in her chest grow to an uncomfortable pace. Long before the Salem witch trials, Heinrich Kramer, 15th century cleric, penned—or quilled—the Malleus Maleficarum and set aflame one very short, but cruel, witch hunt.

"Section Three...those bastards!" She jerked away from the book as if expecting the repugnant words to leap off the page and set her ablaze.

Page after page of detailed instructions for gruesome torture—and ghastly illustrations—further drove her need to complete her thesis despite how appalling the topic was. Researching and translating the ancient language brought her the agonizing knowledge that the women accused of practicing witchcraft had no way to escape interrogation, torture, and eventual death. The pain and suffering of these victims afflicted her personally as she absorbed their history.

Glancing over her shoulder at her empty inbox on the monitor, Tessa fiddled with her pentagram necklace like a security blanket and tapped her foot. With a sigh of annoyance, she refocused on the project in front of her, flipping through the pages of the ancient manual.

You have mail. She tensed when she saw the message from

Madame Evangeline. Before taking the leap, she inhaled and composed herself. 1Night Stand's success was critical for so many reasons. She clicked on the email.

Your match has been found and your date has been arranged at the Castillo Resort in Salem, **Massachusetts,** *on the thirty-first day of October. You will attend the Witch's Ball in the Sapphire Ballroom of the hotel.*

Halloween? Salem? Having her date in her hometown lacked the discretion she'd envisioned when she sought the services of Madame Eve. The sudden shrill of her ringing phone made her jump.

"Hello?"

"Hey Tess, any word yet?"

"Hi Jen, I just got her reply." Her heavy shoulders drooped as she settled back into her chair.

"So, when is it? You don't sound very enthused."

"You won't believe this; maybe Madame Evangeline has a sense of humor."

"What?"

"It's booked for Halloween night at the Witch's Ball."

"You're kidding?" Jen's laughter added to the unease settling in the pit of her stomach.

"Yup, sending a Wiccan to the Witch's Ball to get some—how the hell am I going to keep this discreet? Everyone in town will be there."

"Oh, Tess, try not to worry. Just because they're there doesn't mean they'll know it's an arranged date. Meet him there and then take him somewhere else for the evening."

"Madame Eve has the night planned; check in at three o'clock, attend the ball at seven. She made an appointment for us to *indulge in some of the celebrations*, but I have no idea what that means."

"At the Festival of the Dead? I don't imagine it will be a candlelight dinner or anything tame, but tame isn't your style anyway." A snicker resonated in her ear.

"I'm glad you're amused."

"I'll be going to the ball with Johnny so if you run into any problems, I'll be close by."

"Thanks." A halfhearted scoff slipped out as she tilted her leather office chair back and swayed side to side.

"She booked me into a suite. It feels like I'm playing with fire, so close to home."

"Were you expecting to jet set across the world for one night?"

"I guess I hadn't thought about it."

"It's not like it's an arranged marriage, Tess. It's a night of fun, and unless you plan on bumping uglies in the middle of the dance floor, I would venture a guess that your discretion should remain intact, although your integrity may be in question."

"Okay, smart ass, we're good. Tell me about the curriculum this year; how were the changes?"

"I can take a hint. The changes are fine, but it's not the same without you."

"Sure it isn't."

"How long is this sabbatical?"

"I don't know. I need to finish my research and write my thesis."

"I don't understand your obsession with the Salem witch trials, Tess."

"What's to understand? I'm Wiccan. I live in Salem. I'm a generational witch and a descendent of Sarah Good."

"Seriously?"

"Yes, and being a descendent of one of the first women accused of witchcraft in the witch hunts makes it personal for me."

"You never told me that before."

"I didn't know until recently when I explored my family tree and discovered the information."

"What is it you expect to accomplish with the book?"

"It's not just a book. This abomination is—flesh and blood human beings were murdered because of it by using the ridiculous label of 'witch' to silence women who gave authority figures—men—trouble."

"That's so far in the past; what does it matter now?"

Her face growing hot, she ground her teeth, working to keep her fiery, redheaded temper under control—somewhat. She gripped the cordless phone with tense fingers.

"It matters because their deaths shouldn't be in vain."

"I'm not trying to get you riled up, girl. I just worry."

"Well, don't."

"Where did you get the...abomination?"

"It was a stroke of luck—or misfortune, if you can believe it. I stumbled upon this relic in a pile of discarded books from the Salem Museum."

"What do you mean by misfortune?"

"The horrific details are indescribable."

"Tess, have they gotten any more intense?"

"They—what?"

"Your urges, while reading that—book?"

"Maybe it's because I'm so ripe I could fall off the vine." Tessa eyed the volume, its lure nearly drowning out her friend's concern.

"Do you think there's any connection to your research?"

"No, not exactly. The *Malleus Maleficarum* talks a lot about sexuality, but it's not like reading erotica. I don't find it titillating, just—fascinating, and disturbing at the same time. The primitive thinking about women being vulnerable to the devil's influence because of their gender is unreal."

"So the claims that the book incites sexuality in women...?"

"Oh, you know it's a bunch of malarkey."

"Sure, that's what I thought, but then you wanted to get—a one-night stand. You've always been so prudish about who you sleep with."

"No, I haven't."

"You don't think so?"

"Finicky maybe, but look how long it takes me to buy shoes, and they only go on my feet!"

"Ha ha, very funny."

"Now, when I find the right shoes, it doesn't take me long to wear them out." Giving a purr through the phone, she grinned at Jen's momentary silence.

"Eww. Point taken. Knock it off, you vixen."

"I haven't found the right guy—ever, really, and a girl has needs, you know?"

"Of course I know. It's just not like you."

"Are you saying I'm being tempted by the devil, Jen?"

"Call me old school, in Salem. It's just that the book has so much dark history attached to it, I can't dismiss the possibility."

"Wow, are you ever superstitious."

"I think you're right about playing with fire. Try not to get consumed by it, okay?"

"Consumed? Me?" The book's call grew stronger; her fingers teasing at the pages—were they warm? "I'll see where it leads me."

"You mean like to the gates of hell, you heathen?" Jen chuckled.

"Nice, now that's a supportive message, you harlot."

"Okay, seriously though, tell me some of the main points you're basing your thesis on."

She flipped through the hundreds of sticky notes protruding from the ancient text, excited to share her findings.

"*The Malleus Maleficarum* is a living piece of history containing some of the most ridiculous, yet enduring, assumptions about females you'll ever hear." She opened to another page and read the note there. "The treatise describes how '*women become inclined for witchcraft, claiming they were susceptible to demonic temptations through their manifold weaknesses*'. People believed that they were weaker in faith and more carnal than men."

"Manifold weaknesses, my word."

"Even today, in rape trials or domestic assaults, men still refute their responsibility citing she asked for it. Look at how she's dressed, how she walks, her hair was down—she breathed."

"Don't you think modern society has gotten better with that?"

"Maybe some, but the underlying message of women owning responsibility for bewitching a man because they can't keep it in their pants is still there."

"I can see your point. The trouble with your research and thesis, my dear friend, is how time consuming and isolating it can become. I haven't seen you in three weeks." Jen's voice tightened, revealing her worry.

"I hear ya. I need to get my head clear. I'm done outlining it now—a little more research and maybe a small experiment...."

"What are you talking about?"

"This date. It's about sex anyway, so I'm going all out. I'm gonna do everything and not worry about the consequences."

"You're kidding."

"No, I'm not. It's a one-night stand. He'll be there for the same reason, more or less, and I'll never have to see him again. I'll take precautions."

"Sounds like the makings of a real happily ever after."

"I already told you, *happily ever after* is not in my future, but a happy right now might be. At least this way I can test my theory about bewitching and tempting a mortal man."

"What is *that* supposed to mean—are you casting a spell on him?"

"Figuratively speaking, maybe. With my wanton body only, though, no potions or chanting." The sides of her mouth drew up at her own humor.

"Oh my God, you're such a tramp."

"At least I hope to be." They both laughed.

"Fair enough, now get back to work. We'll go costume hunting together this weekend, maybe find something sexy for the occasion?"

"Sexy for the later part of the night, sure, but something fitting for the Witch's Ball. It's a deal. See you Saturday."

Chapter Two

"Samson, I assure you, no one will know about this arrangement."

"Jacob, I appreciate your support and your discretion, but I feel like a hypocrite. The old *do as I say and not as I do* doesn't sit well, not with me, and not with my parish." Easing back into the hardness of the squeaky oak chair, he folded his hands on his lap.

"What they don't know—"

"I'll know. That isn't proper leadership."

"Even men of the church have needs. Being a pastor does not condemn you to celibacy." The graying man sat across the desk with a confident gaze. "Even a senior pastor, such as myself...."

Samson's heart skipped a beat. "Jacob? You used the service?"

"Yes, Madame Eve and I go way back."

"What about your wife? Abigail would be—"

"Let's just say, it happened before she and I were together, and one night of indiscretion has rewarded me with ten years of wonderful marriage." Studying Jacob's sly grin, he caught on to his subtlety.

"Abigail, really?"

"The luckiest night of my life."

"What about the importance of—relations—we discuss with

our parish?"

"Being a community leader has its share of responsibilities, yes. Personal abstinence isn't one of them."

"No, but sex without love—" Resting his elbow on the arm of the chair, he soothed his aching temple with his fingers.

"Gratifying your needs doesn't reflect a personal disregard for the virtues you bestow upon your parishioners. Think of it this way—do you lay claim that one's physical desires make him dark and unnatural?" Jacob leaned forward over the desk, appealing to him with knitted brows.

"Of course not."

"Why not?"

"It's human nature to have urges."

"Is that what you tell your parishioners?" Jacob's challenging tone was matched with his empathetic gaze.

"Yes, but I also give guidance about self-respect and that promiscuity is not...."

"Not?"

"Not the Christian way." Samson straightened, his shoulders stiff with tension.

"Are you expecting to engage in harmful behavior during an interlude?"

"No, I would never harm another."

"I know you wouldn't. That's the message that is most important." His elderly confidant settled back into the chair with a gentle smile. "It's a date, Samson. Dating is allowed."

"Sure it is, but this date has a pre-determined outcome."

"Meeting a lovely lady for a date is not a sin. Whatever happens throughout the course of the night will be your decision at that time, not a moment before."

"I haven't any answers left, Jacob." Samson shook his head, exhaling with frustration.

"Let me put it another way. In all the years I've been your mentor, do you feel I have deceived you, misled you, or become a dark and negative influence in any way?"

"No, I would never say that."

"So you would not condemn me for one night of indiscretion?"

"No, absolutely not." Samson furrowed his brows in response to the ludicrous question.

"Well then, it's settled."

"What is?"

"You would not condemn me, nor I you, my friend. As your mentor and your spiritual leader, I am abolishing any judgment on you for seeking to meet your needs for this one night. During your date, you are not a pastor of this church. You, sir, will be a flesh and blood human being, seeking to have his urges satisfied. That's it." Jacob's weathered grin lit up his smiling blue eyes.

"I can't argue with that, I suppose."

With a heavy heart, Samson swung his noisy, wooden office chair around and hit the *send* button.

"You won't regret it, I assure you, as your friend."

Feeling a little lighter, Samson shook his head in partial agreement.

"There is one stipulation, however."

"What's that?" Letting a one-sided grin escape, he anticipated what Jacob would say next.

"It is paramount that you take the time to enjoy yourself. This is a chance to be free of the confines of your religious inhibitions. You will be a better man for it, I guarantee. The Lord works in mysterious ways, and for that matter, so does Eve."

Chapter Three

She flipped her black canvas bag open on the bathroom counter and fished through its contents. Bypassing the shaving cream, she propped up her foot on the side of the tub and inspected her smooth, hairless leg. The esthetician in the salon downstairs had done an excellent pampering job. Waxing, facial, manicure, pedicure. No need for excess grooming, just a nice hot shower in her luxurious suite and then slip into her costume.

Taking out her small array of candles and incense, she inhaled deeply, cherishing the woody patchouli and lavender fragrances. Eyeing the telling red light on the smoke detector, she clicked on the ceiling fan to mask the smoke and set her earthy tools for relaxation alight. Turn on the water, switch off the light, and she had the makings for a soothing shower.

She peeled off her heavy, rustic knit sweater and skinny jeans and stepped into the black marble cubicle. The heated water splashing down soothed her tense body. The anxiety-ridden lead up to tonight had taken a toll on her muscles. A complimentary bottle of body wash on the shelf appealed to her, so she grabbed a cloth and lathered up with the lemon balm scented potion.

"Ahh." The flickering light of the candles shimmered along the gleaming walls and steam soon filled the spacious bathroom. Wisps of patchouli floated past her nose. She had officially arrived in heaven.

"Excuse me?" A deep voice cut through the serenity of her steamy oasis.

She screamed and reached through the curtain, grabbing the nearest towel and draping it across her soapy body. Ready to face whatever invaded her tranquility, she yanked the shower curtain open.

"What the hell?"

"I didn't mean to startle you, but what are you doing in my suite?" Through the candlelit mist, she saw the silhouette of a man waving what appeared to be a room card.

"Yours? This is my suite." She clutched the white terry cloth like a lifeline, while suds dripped down her face. Her heart thudded with ferocious force as she worked to catch her breath and fumbled with the tap. First, a torrent of scalding hot water shocked her then she turned the knob the other way, and instant icing encased her trembling body. Shutting the water off, she glared at the mysterious figure while securing the towel under her arms.

"There must be a mistake. I had—reservations made on my behalf." His voice softened a little though she couldn't get a look at his face, as he remained cloaked by steam. Flustered, she stepped out of the shower.

"No kidding, a mistake." Her cheeks growing hot, she stepped forward. As the air began to clear and the stranger's face emerged her soapy, wet feet slipped across the cold marble. With a shriek, she flew forward and braced for impact, but instead of crashing to the floor, she landed in his arms.

"Whoa, I got ya." He held tight. Her shock was outweighed by the erratic pounding of her heart against the confines of her terry-covered chest; gasping for air, she stared up at his remarkable golden brown eyes.

"I'm fine. You can let go now." Pushing away from his chest, she reached her feet to the floor, trying to escape his grasp. When her toes barely touched the wet surface and she tried to steady herself, she slid again. Easing her onto the safety of the mat, he stepped back. He kept his gaze on the card in his fumbling fingers, avoiding her venomous glare.

Despite her irritation with his presence in her private suite, she took a closer look at his striking face and broad shoulders. A clean shaven man with salt and pepper hair, chiseled features, full lips, and smooth, flawless skin. Clad in faded blue jeans that molded to his lean thighs and a button-down denim shirt, she found him remarkably handsome, in an annoying way, of course. The faded brown cowboy boots didn't hurt either.

ೞ

"I am sorry for the confusion, Ms. Ledger and Mr. Langley. The reservation would appear to be correct."

"For two?" Tessa's irritation was exacerbated by her wavy wet strands dripping water down her forehead.

"Yes, in both your names."

"Who made the reservation?" His deep, smooth voice distracted her from her intended bludgeoning of the concierge.

"One moment, please." The clerk typed away on his keyboard, staring at the monitor.

"I can't seem to find that information. The reservation was made in-house by Mr. Castillo from our flagship resort in Las Vegas. I can call him if you like?"

Tessa chewed on her lower lip. Her suite was part of the package she'd booked through 1Night Stand. Along with the date, who must be...? She sighed.

"Shall I change the reservations?" The young concierge glanced between Tessa and her stranger.

"No—uh—yes—uh, can you please give us a minute? Come here." She grabbed the stranger's wrist and guided him to the side.

"Let's just take a second here and catch our breath." He eased her clenched fingers off his wrist.

"Oh, I'm sorry. I guess I got a little worked up."

"A little." One side of his mouth curled up, sending a flush of warmth and frustration shooting through her.

"What is your name, anyway?"

"I'm Samson. And you are? "His devilishly charming grin lit up his face.

"Tessa."

"It's a pleasure to meet you." Like a gentleman, he raised her hand to his lips and kissed the back of her fingers.

"We can't—it's not private down here." Tessa pulled away. "We should go back upstairs to talk about this." Scanning the vast lobby of the resort for any familiar faces, she straightened her shoulders and gave him a stern glare.

"That's fine, let's go." He waved her ahead of him toward the elevator.

"Will that be all?" the concierge stared from one to the other, looking worried.

Tessa glared at the gangly man and nodded briefly.

The man who was—apparently—her date for the evening, ushered her into the narrow compartment.

Chapter Four

The *Do Not Disturb* sign dangled from the outside handle as Tessa pushed the heavy door closed and secured the entrance. The sound of the clicking lock sent a spasm of nerves through her chest.

"I'm confused. Are you not interested in having a—date—with me?" Samson walked to the bathroom, grabbed a dry towel, and passed it to her.

"Of course I am. Why would you think that?" She rubbed the fluffy material through her dripping hair.

"You seem, I don't know...tense." He sat down on the king sized bed and watched while she dried her locks with frantic hands.

"You think? If I had known we were sharing a room, we wouldn't have had to broadcast our sleeping arrangements in the lobby for everyone to hear."

"I see." He nodded.

"Why do you look so smug?"

"I do?" With knitted brows, he caught her gaze.

"Maybe you don't need to be discreet, but I live in this town, and I don't want anyone to find out I'm using a dating service."

"Perhaps we need to clarify something. I need as much discretion as you do, if not more."

"More?" The display of anger grew tiresome, and she realized she could lose her chance for frolicking if she kept up the disgruntled redhead bit much longer. Taking in a deep breath then exhaling, Tessa sat down on the end of the plush mattress. She twisted and twirled the corner of the damp towel while she eyed him more directly.

"I live close by as well, and my line of work—"

"What do you do?"

"I'm a—community leader. I have to maintain appropriate decorum for the people who seek my guidance." He heaved a sigh and looked to the side with pursed lips.

"That's pretty vague. Are you married or something? Are you looking for a quickie affair?" Her unease started to gain momentum.

"Heavens no."

Reclaiming eye contact, she searched his face for any hint of deception and saw none. "I'm not expecting anything past this evening; you don't have to worry about me becoming some needy cling-on that expects a wedding band or anything."

"I'm not concerned about anything like that."

"Then what is it?"

"I have always worked to set a positive example for my community. If anyone finds out about this—interlude—I may lose their respect."

"Sweet Jesus, you sound like a priest or something." She snickered.

The sudden raising of his brows and flaring of his nostrils sent a shock wave through her stomach.

"Oh no, no, no.... Are you?" Inching away in discomfort, she rambled on. "Because if you are, there is no way I'm going to—"

"No, I'm not a priest. I'm not sworn to celibacy."

"But...?"

Biting his lower lip, he looked to the side, avoiding her eyes. "I am a pastor. This is embarrassing for me."

"Samson, is it?" Tessa edged closer to him.

"Yes."

"Please don't be embarrassed. This isn't something I would

normally do either."

"It isn't?"

"Of course not." She paused and steadied her voice. "It's only—one night." Placing her hand over his, she squeezed a little and canvassed his glum expression.

"Yes, one night." The residual disgrace in his expression faded when he looked directly at her and tightened his grip, returning the supportive gesture.

"Are you embarrassed or ashamed?" Curiosity made her ask. *It seems so strange for a pastor to seek out a one-night stand. Why would he do it?*

"Is there a difference?"

"Actually, there is. Embarrassment is uneasiness or humiliation, shame happens when you believe you're doing something wrong." She watched carefully for signs of...of, well she didn't know what. Anything in is face that belied his words, but nothing showed but clear honesty in his handsome features.

"You're right." His eyes narrowed a little.

"Do you think this is wrong, to be with me tonight?"

Samson straightened his shoulders up and drew in a slow, deep breath. "No, for this date, I am a flesh and blood person, not a man of the church."

"Good because I'm eager to get started on our date." She moved her hand to his denim covered leg.

Faced with such a good-looking man, her determination to follow through with her agenda solidified. Thesis or no thesis, she had to have some personal limits to her research, albeit not many.

"Okay, I'm pretty sure that's something I can live with." Easing sideways, he faced her and brushed the damp strands of hair off her forehead. "You are one beautiful lady. Tessa, is it?"

"It is." She leaned her cheek into the warmth of his palm and dropped her towel to the floor.

"You know, I didn't get to finish my shower earlier." She smoothed the residual soap film along her hair, grimacing. "I wouldn't mind jumping back into the hot water—would you care to—join me?" Getting straight to the point was awkward but necessary.

"Don't we have to go to the ball soon?" His gaze wandered from her damp hair, down the length of her loose russet sweater.

"That's easy enough; I already had a wake-up call booked for six-thirty, in case I lost track of time." Working her best husky voice and seductive smile, she eyed him with anticipation. Intense yearning swept over her body as she watched his striking eyes and handsome face.

"I—uh—I—" Stammering, Samson inched his way back a little, and she sighed.

"I'm being too aggressive. I'm sorry; I didn't mean to make you uncomfortable." She turned on the mattress toward the bathroom, tired of being sticky with soap and completely out of feminine wiles.

"It's not that—please don't apologize." He reached out, grabbing her hand again.

"Then what is it?"

"I haven't—done—it's been a really long time for me." Samson's cheeks grew bright red then he faced away from her.

"Oh." Relieved, she treaded carefully.

"I hope you're not—" His inability to complete a sentence became somewhat endearing.

"I'm not, it's okay. I'm gonna hop in the shower and get the soap out of my hair. No pressure, we have all night." Tessa stood up trying to appear nonchalant, easing her hand out from under his, and walked to her suitcase under the window.

"I'll bet this is the worst date you've ever had." A heavy sigh followed his words.

"No, don't be silly. Let's get ready for the ball. A little time to settle in and get comfortable may be a good thing for both of us." Lying to a pastor, the first step of her journey to the gates of Hell.

"Do you drink wine?" Her voice cracked.

"Yes. Would you like me to order room service?"

"That would be great; I'll freshen up." Tessa opened the suitcase feeling self-conscious.

"Sounds good." While he called down for service, Tessa fumbled through the four different negligees she had brought to choose from. *What do I put on now? Too early for the ball ensemble and a nightie is going to send him screaming out into the hallway.*

As she rummaged through her things, her fingers brushed over the heavy book at the bottom of the suitcase.

Seducing a normal, willing man was one thing, but seducing a pastor? Her original plan hadn't worked, too aggressive. What if she tried again and he lost interest altogether? This ironic twist held an appealing challenge, but the morality attached to having casual sex with a man of the church felt uncanny at best. Talk about putting an edge to her research.

ભ

Tessa undressed in the bathroom and left the door ajar; was that too forward?

The joy-gasm of the stream of hot water down her flustered body for the second time was anticlimactic. Maybe she should switch it to cold and simmer down on the sexual conquest issue.

Flickering candlelight glowed through the white linen shower curtain as she rinsed the soap away and tried to relax her body and mind. This was going to be a long night—she had to rethink everything. Maybe her research would be pointless with this particular adventure.

"Excuse me, Tessa?" The deep voice startled her.

"Yes?" She blinked, afraid to move and scare him away again

"May I ask an unusual favor?"

"What is it?"

"May I open the curtain?"

What? She peeked out the side at him.

"You want it open?"

"If it's all right, I would like to—look at you." The sheepish tone of his voice and the innocence of his raised brows made her smile. She pushed the white barrier to the side covering her breasts with an arm. A tremor in her thighs began, coupled with the slight clatter of her teeth. A cold draft enveloped her skin in the absence of the linen partition, bringing a mass of goose bumps to the surface.

"Okay." Pulling her shoulders back and lowering her arm, she lifted her chin and stood still. His inquisitive eyes quested along her exposed flesh while the heat of the cascading water swathed her.

"You're beautiful." The corners of his mouth pulled back revealing a charismatic, devious expression like the cat that swallowed the canary. Cunning and sly.

"Thank you."

I'm glad he thinks so. Be cool, don't overreact—maybe this night will work out after all.

"May I—touch you?" His focus fell back down to her chest.

"You know, we can save ourselves a lot of time tonight."

"How?"

"Let's just be clear. You have my permission, for the remainder of our date, to touch, feel, ogle, and enjoy my body at will. You don't need to ask permission for every action."

A one sided grin emerged as he nodded and began to unbutton his denim shirt.

"Understood." As he let the garment fall from his shoulders, it was her turn to inspect, and she liked what she saw.

"Wow." She studied the sculpted planes of his chest and abdomen. His lean, muscular physique had been well hidden beneath his casual attire. The broad shoulders she had already noticed were solid and strong; his arms rock-hard and chiseled, making this man the perfect specimen for her night of seduction.

The clinking of his unbuckling belt brought a stir to her core while she watched. Anticipation climbed as he unbuttoned his tight jeans, and unzipped, then tugged them down, revealing his magnificent and tantalizing dick.

She stepped back, making room as her soon-to-be conquest joined her, and stood facing him with the water pouring down her back. "I thought I spooked you."

His caress on her shoulder and down the length of her arm induced a giddy sensation that overtook her shivering body.

"Spooked? On Halloween? That's funny." Retracing his way back up her arm and across her neck, his warm fingers followed the path of the flowing water down her chest and stopped just above her aroused peaks.

"May I?" She rested her palm against his cheek without waiting for his reply.

"Of course. You don't need to ask permission either. Sky's the limit, my lady." He smoothed her hand down his virile chest and hard, sleek stomach in a slow but firm motion. Elated, she worshiped his steely contours with stroking fingers.

Samson's hungry eyes penetrated hers, as he stood silent and intense. He left her hand to travel on its own and cupped her face in his wet palms, staring at her.

Her heart raced and her chest tightened as she awaited his next move. Grazing her lips, he kept just enough distance that she could barely feel his breath. Her fingers trailed down to his rigid hard on and she massaged it with anticipation.

At a loud knock at the door, her elusive prey pulled back with a smile while she stared at him with desperation.

"I ordered room service. I forgot about it." He grabbed a towel and wrapped it around his waist on his way to the door. The sudden chill of goose bumps erupted again, followed by the clatter of her teeth in disbelief. So close, she had been so close, *dammit.*

Chapter Five

A bottle of chardonnay and half a tray of **hors d'oeuvres** later, she began to feel brave, or maybe even brazen. Tessa sauntered up to her target wearing her crimson satin negligee. She placed her half-empty glass of wine on the nightstand, led her object of desire across the room, and urged him to sit on the edge of the bed.

Pulling the smooth material up her thighs, she eased herself into his lap, straddling him, and wrapped her arms around his neck, studying his face. Her mounting attraction had set off a fiery intensity of yearning, making her eager to tantalize him. She was determined the previous coitus interuptus be but a delay in her sexual gratification on this all Hallows' Eve.

The heat of his palms stroking the small of her back spurred her on. The speed of her pulse increased and intense warmth washed over her body as she settled on his thighs, fitting over his growing erection. Initiating the closeness with him felt almost forced because she had an agenda. Gliding her hands back from his neck, she cradled his face as she gathered her courage, staring into the chocolate brown of his compelling gaze.

Samson's hands slid up and caressed along her shoulders then to her face. His dark, ravenous stare brought a stir to her core as he gripped her tight. Pulling her to him, he devoured her with an impassioned kiss. Her lips parted slightly, welcoming the entry of his sweeping tongue. Responding to his heat and passion, she ground her pelvis against his growing hardness.

Blazing a trail of kisses down this throat, she reveled in his woody, spicy fragrance—like sweet mahogany and nutmeg. More confident now, she intertwined her fingers in his thick, luscious hair, satisfaction filling her when a low groan emerged from the bottom of his throat.

He tightened his arms around her waist, stood and swung her around, dropping her onto her back on the bed. She had wondered if he would be meek and shy given his profession. She had convinced herself she would have to be the aggressor, but the man before her was every inch the alpha male as he tore open the hotel robe he had put on earlier, dropping it on the floor.

Like a panther to its prey, he eased his way on top of her and stroked her mouth to ecstasy with his tongue. Exploring the length of her satin-covered body with his powerful fingers, he pulled the spaghetti straps off her shoulders, freeing her breasts.

A gasp of bliss slipped out at the exquisite heated tongue whisking one engorged peak while he rolled the other between his fingers.

Samson leaned back and gazed at her with a sexy grin. "My God, you're gorgeous." He kneaded and stroked her taut flesh.

"You're not so bad yourself." Cupping her hand over his, she squeezed his fingers tighter, shuddering in pleasure. He recaptured her lips, and her core clenched as his rock hard cock rubbed over the inside of her thigh. Running her fingers along the bunching muscles of his shoulders, she dug her into the taut skin of his back, urging him even closer while their tongues danced. Samson eased her thighs apart and slid her panties down and off.

His fingers explored the outer layers of her fleshy folds. Breaking the kiss, he brought his finger to his mouth and tasted it. He slid his hand down to her pussy again and massaged her throbbing clit in slow, torturous circles.

"Oh." She gasped and stretched her arms above her head, sprawled out on the luxurious bed, at the mercy of her rogue man of the cloth.

Sliding his palm down farther, he parted the throbbing flesh and pushed a finger deep into her pussy.

Lost in the sensations, it took a moment for her psyche to realize the shrilling noise that shattered their mood was the phone.

"Oh no, you have got to be kidding." She groaned. "There must be a greater force at work; this is the second interruption."

"Hold that thought." He reached over her and grabbed the ringing unit from the bedside table.

"Hello?"

Working to control her panting breath, she focused on the pulsing still contracting her core. *So close.*

"Yes, thank you." He hung up but did not return to pleasing Tessa.

"Our wake-up call?"

"I'm afraid so. It's already six thirty, and our table at the ball is reserved and waiting for us."

"It would be okay if we skipped it, wouldn't it?" She pouted and rolled on her side to look into his eyes.

With a soft laugh, he shook his head. "Sorry Tessa, it's unavoidable. Madame Evangeline booked us for some evening activities and we are expected to make an appearance."

"Good Lord, is this a sign or something?" She sat up, pulling her negligee back into place.

"Well, I'm not quite sure about that, although it does make me wonder. Come on, the sooner we go—"

"The sooner we can get back and come." She grinned at him then ducked her head as her cheeks heated. *Not as bold as I'd like to think, sometimes.*

"Now that *was* funny."

"Who said I was kidding?" Tessa hopped off the bed and moved to the closet.

"I—I'm speechless."

"Apparently I have that effect on people at times."

Chapter Six

*T*ess approached the entrance to the Sapphire Ballroom arm in arm with her handsome escort. Brushing aside a heavy black velvet curtain, they stepped into a world of dark and eerie ambiance with the flickering flames of dozens of wrought iron torches that lit the ceiling draped with glowing nettings of simulated spider webs. She cringed at morbid displays of guillotines, executioners, dripping fake blood, and disembodied limbs. Dozens of luminescent jack-o-lanterns lit the way, filling the air with the smell of scorched pumpkin.

Tessa squinted through the dry ice fog at the labyrinth of tables covered with black cloths and decked with flickering candle lit centerpieces encircling the massive dance floor.

"How do we find our table?" She turned in circles, stunned by the rectangular bales of hay, dried corn stalks, and every imaginable Halloween cliché from skeletons to vampires throughout the venue.

"What are these booths?" His deep velvet voice so close to her ear sent a thrill down her spine. She regained control of herself and noticed he was pointing to the various vendor tables lining the walls.

"It would seem that Salem has yet again embraced the traditional folklore of fortune tellers, spell casters, and magic potions." Trying to conceal her disdain, Tessa motioned over to the makeshift bar featuring multi-colored glass beakers of smoking, bubbling concoctions. The bartender, wearing a voodoo witch doctor outfit including a big bone in his nose, dropped straws into the smoking brews he distributed to patrons.

Dry ice mist spilled out of every conceivable hidden nook throughout the ballroom, under tables, in the bubbling glass centerpieces, and even in the hanging cauldrons set center stage. The continuous fog emitted a cooling sensation, adding to the chilly and creepy ambience of the evening. Until now, Tessa's recall of the day being Halloween had been in the background as she focused being on a more carnal conquest.

"What's that on the stage?" Samson pointed to a massive black tent. A cloaked person sitting at the covered entranceway collected admission to the mysterious attraction. With the crowd's chatter muffled by the haunted sounds of rattling chains, sinister laughter, howls, and screams, it most definitely felt like Halloween.

"I'm not sure; there's no sign up. It is spooky looking though." Tessa's distaste for the décor lightened a little at the smile of amusement on her date's face.

"There's our table." She tugged him toward the eerie sign bearing their names in an impressive bloodied font. "We're sharing with others. Thirteen seats here."

"Would you like a drink?" he asked, pulling out her chair.

"Yes, thank you." She slipped into the chair, glancing around to see if any of their tablemates might be approaching. Theirs was the only table without a full complement of merrymakers in outlandish costumes.

"Anything in particular?"

"Oh, I don't know, maybe a bloody Mary?"

"Nice." He chuckled and walked over to the bar.

Inspecting the empty chairs and place settings around the table, she noticed none of their tablemates had arrived, but she did observe something strange. The name cards bore familiar names: *Dorcas (Dorothy) Good, Ann Putnam, Jr., Magistrate John Hawthorne. Several more followed, each a significant figure during the trials.*

Samson and Tessa's cards stated their given and surnames, with a blank space underneath, appearing incomplete. The others had titles under their names, Witch, Magistrate, but not theirs.

At their place setting, waited a manila envelope.

"Here you go." Samson returned and placed a black and red drink in front of her. "They were out of bloody Mary mix, so I got you a Devil's Blood cocktail. Hope this is okay."

"Ah—yes, thank you."

"What's wrong—you don't like this? I can get something else."

"No, no, this is fine, thanks."

"What is it?" He faced her with probing eyes.

"I don't think anyone else is sitting here." She pointed to the nametags.

"No?"

"These names are all people associated with the Salem Witch Trials in 1692." A slight hint of bile rose at the back of her throat.

"Just Halloween humor, I guess." He rubbed her back, where her muscles had knotted as she read the place cards.

"I guess." She shook her head and shrugged her shoulders to dislodge her unease. "Enough with the gruesome stuff. Can I ask you a question?"

"You just did."

"Funny."

"I thought so. What is it?" He took a sip of his drink as he watched her.

"Why on earth did you decide to wear a priest costume?"

"You mean the devil priest?" He patted the plastic horns on his head, stroked the fake, black goatee glued to his chin, and then leered at her.

"Well, yes." She sat back a little sizing him up with a dismayed stare.

"I thought it would be amusing, making light of my— indiscretion. Maybe it was in poor taste." He settled back into his chair, seeming a little deflated as his shoulders dropped down.

"No, maybe...I don't know. It just seemed...weird."

"May I ask *you* a question now?"

"Sure." Shrugging, Tessa sat back and lifted the glass to sip from the straw. A sudden shot of sour shock shot through her mouth at the bitter sweetness of the cranberry and black vodka mix. *You'd think I could get a bloody Mary at a Halloween ball...or maybe everyone had the same idea and drank it all up. This is...odd.* She flushed realizing Samson stared, waiting for her attention. "Oh, go ahead and ask."

"What's with the cut rope hanging around your neck, and the peasant outfit?"

"Actually, I am supposed to be Sarah Good, from the witch trials. Dead Sarah, anyway."

"Oh, that's—morbid."

"It is Samhain." She sipped again, and the tart sweetness of the drink grew on her.

"What's that?"

"The Witch's New Year, Halloween, a Wiccan Sabbat."

"Does that mean you're Wiccan?"

"If I said yes, would that be a problem?" Her defenses surfaced.

"Of course not. It just didn't occur to me that we would be—of different faiths."

"Good thing it's a one-night stand and not a marriage proposal."

"What's that in your hand?"

"It's for us. I haven't opened it yet."

He took the envelope and tore it open.

"Ah, now we know what the big black tent is."

"What?"

"These are passes for a complimentary séance." With furrowed brow, and lips pressed tight, he gave the card back to her.

"You seem disturbed."

"No, not really; it's just, I've always talked to God, but not the dead, so to speak."

"I'm guessing it's just a hoax, or gimmick, but this is supposed to be the most magical night for communicating with the dead."

"Why is that?"

"Because on Samhain—Halloween—the veil between the living and the dead is at its thinnest, making speaking with the dead that much more possible."

"That sounds kind of creepy."

"It starts in ten minutes." When she stood and moved toward the stage, he followed.

Chapter Seven

Sitting at the black velour sheathed table, he took in the evocative set up. A crystal ball on a pewter snake stand in the middle of a gold, iron-on pentagram. Dozens of flickering red candles sheathed with melted wax surrounded the poignant centerpiece. Still, determined to go where the evening took him, he joined Tess and the other guests already seated around the table.

"Tess? Oh my God." Soft laughter drew his attention to the black-and-white striped convict couple, attached by a linked chain around their necks, entering the tent.

"Jen? Johnny? I don't believe it." Tessa sank down into her seat, as the blonde woman kissed her on the cheek

"So Tessa, who is your—friend?"

"Ah—Jen, Johnny, this is Samson." Tessa spoke in a soft, shaky voice.

"It's good to meet you both." Standing with a smile, he reached across the table to shake their hands.

"Thank you for joining us on this magical night." A sultry voice drifted over the group as a tall woman made a dramatic entrance, flinging the sides of her deep purple velvet cape back over her shoulders. Straight strands of jet-black hair cascaded across her shoulders and down her chest. She wore a black lace, ribbed corset, which forced the protrusion of her pale breasts into exceptional and pronounced cleavage. Samson couldn't help but sit back down with a fixed stare and gaping jaw.

Tessa eased his hanging mouth closed with narrowed eyes and a sarcastic smirk. "Down, boy."

"Excuse me." His cheeks grew hot when he caught her fierce glare, and he hurried to put his arm around her.

"My name is Madame Raven, and I will be your host for the séance tonight. I am a psychic, clairvoyant, channel, and medium." Madame primped up her corset and sat down with pronounced movements. Suspended over her brazenly exposed cleavage dangled an ornate pentagram on a silver chain, and on the swell of her right breast a colored triquatra tattoo. He'd only seen the design in books before—he'd have so much to share with Jacob after this extraordinary evening.

"Please join hands round the table." Madame Raven talked the group through a brief meditation, not much different from a prayer he might offer during a sermon, getting them all into the haunted feel of the moment. In his prayers, he spoke to only one God, straightforward and not confusing, but this lady called on a variety of deities. *What a fascinating experience, rather like a trip to a mission in a far off land!*

"I feel we are blessed on this All Hallows Eve. Spirit is strong with us and eager to speak. Whatever happens, do not break this sacred circle. Remain holding hands until we close the circle at the end."

He smiled to see Tessa roll her eyes as the medium spoke—at least they shared an opinion of this charlatan.

Madame's head drooped and her body remained still for several minutes. He glanced around the group and stifled a sarcastic laugh at the other guests' rapt attention on their hostess. Jen held Madame's left hand while a male guest grasped the other. Tessa and Samson sat across from her, front row seat for the show. Abruptly, the psychic's head popped up. She glared at Tessa with her bright green eyes wide open and spoke in a higher voice than her husky sound earlier.

"Tessa? Is that you dear?"

"What?" He could hear the grinding of Tessa's teeth as she shot a fiery glare at the woman. "Funny, Madame Raven. Maybe you should focus on someone else."

"Darling, it's me, your mother."

Her fingers gripped tighter around his and her cheeks grew crimson. "Cut it out, that's not funny. Jen, did you put her up to this?"

"What? No Tess, I swear." Her voice cracked and was almost a whisper.

He watched the women's heated exchange, uneasy and ready to bolt, dragging Tessa by the arm if necessary. "What's going on?"

"Daughter, my time is short. You wear the necklace I gave you during your dedication ceremony on your sixteenth birthday."

Tessa's expression went flat. "No one knows about that." The droplets spilled down her cheeks as she faced the psychic.

"Yes, my daughter, it's me. Tessa, your ancestor is here to warn you of danger."

Madame Eva's body shifted, as she squinted then went wide-eyed.

"Tessa Dorcas Ledger, I command thee."

"Who is that?" Samson whispered. He was confused but realized the medium wasn't faking this. Something very real and very eerie was happening.

"I am Sarah Good. Tessa, you bring danger to yourself with the book."

"Sarah Good is your ancestor?" he hissed.

She nodded.

"What book?" He asked, louder this time.

Tessa didn't move; her crimson cheeks faded to pale white.

"You must banish this book. The longer you have it in your possession, the greater the draw of the dark and unnatural." The room was growing stagnant from the heat of the burning candles, the air warm. Perspiration began to form on his forehead. The flames grew tall and flickered wildly.

"But my research—"

"I command you to obey, Tessa Ledger, or your fate will equal mine."

"My fate?"

"I do not have much time. I grow weaker by the moment."

"Sarah, please, were you...what they accused you of?" A torrent of tears flooded Tessa's cheeks.

"I was but a hungry, sad, and lonely woman. I begged for food. I had no pillow for my head and nothing to offer my starving children. The townspeople were cruel and uncaring. They told horrible lies to punish me for my imprudence. The men that demanded favors for food took revenge at my denials to them, and their wives spurned me because of their husbands' turning heads."

"Were you a witch, Sarah?"

Samson couldn't believe his senses. Did he face the ghost of Sarah Goode, executed for witchcraft over three hundred years before?

"What you know now as a witch is vastly different than my accusers proclaimed."

"I don't understand?" Tessa pleaded, leaning across the table toward the medium—psychic—ghost?

"Your generation sees the healing in the craft, the herbs and potions. You come from a long line of women of strength and courage, a line denounced by any man they crossed. The danger you attract on this night Tessa, is that of tempting a direct descendent of the one who convicted me, the one who condemned my children—the one who brought death to my infant." Glaring eyes and shaking fingers pointed at Samson.

"What?" His back stiffened and his grip on her fingers tightened.

"You." She pointed at him again. "The descendent of John Hawthorn." Her shriek rose over the gathering and a searing white heat washed over his body.

Tessa stared at him with wide eyes.

"You're from the Hawthorn bloodline?"

"No one is supposed to know that." His teeth clenched.

"You're of his blood and you preach good will to people? You hypocrite." She yanked at her hand, but he tightened his grip.

"Wait a minute. I'm not him, Tessa."

Madame's body shook and her head dropped to her chest again.

"I can't do this, not with you."

Madame rose to her feet and spoke in a commanding voice. "Tessa, the book, you must be rid of it forever." Madame or Sarah dropped with a heavy thud into the chair. She let out a big exhale and laid her head on the table. Despite her movement, no one broke the circle.

Samson searched the horrified faces and surveyed the gripped hands of the people around the table, realizing the impact this was having on everyone. His stomach turned as he witnessed the whites of their knuckles almost glowing under the candlelight.

Tessa's eyes flitted around the table. Fuming and disturbed, he squeezed her hand so tight that she flinched under his grip.

"What book?" He demanded.

"It's none of your business." She glared at him with malice and jerked her hands free, pushing the chair back with such force, it crashed to the floor.

"Tess. Where are you going?" Jen asked.

"I've had enough of this." Tessa stormed out of the tent.

Chapter Eight

Rifling through her bag in a frenzy, Tessa grabbed her jeans and sweater she'd worn earlier and rushed into the bathroom to change, hoping to disappear before having to face him again. Anger and fear washed over her body and her trembling hands fumbled with her garments. At the mirror, she removed the rope from her neck and then jerked with fright at a reflection beside hers. A glance to her right confirmed she stood alone in front of the glass, and she focused again on the mirror. A pale, desolate woman in similar attire, with a frayed rope cutting into the skin of her neck. In disbelief, Tessa shook her head and the vision disappeared. Running the cold water and splashing her face, she tried to wake from her terrifying shock. The welling of tears returned, and she brushed them away with the back of her hand. The red rims of her eyes highlighted her swollen lids, smeared with black makeup, her image was comparable to something from a bad horror movie.

She pulled off her costume and slipped into her clothes. She then gathered her things and rushed out of the bathroom only to find Samson sitting on the bed—holding the Malleus Maleficarum. His jaw hung open and his face was filled with worry.

"What in God's name are you doing with this, Tessa?"

"You went through my bag? How dare you?" She stomped over and tried to take it from him.

"When Sarah mentioned the book, I couldn't even imagine she meant this." He refused to let go. "Why don't you try telling me what the hell these notes mean, huh?" He pulled out her step-by-step plan to seduce her one-night stand.

"Give me that—you have no right."

He grabbed her wrist, stopping her from touching the book. "I don't? What gives you the right? You planned a seduction based on the evil workings of this abomination for fun? What? Was tonight just for kicks?" She remained silent "Answer me."

"I've been writing a thesis. I didn't mean any harm."

"A thesis? That's why you set this night up? On Halloween?"

"I didn't plan the date."

"What exactly *did* you plan? Were you thinking of casting this spell of lust on me, too?" He pulled out more notes.

"No, of course not, that was just research."

"Research."

"What about you? Mr. Descendent of the Magistrate John Hawthorn, were you looking for a witch to condemn?"

"All right, that's enough." He released her wrist.

"Why is your last name different? Were you trying to hide your agenda?"

"My grandfather changed his surname to get away from this history. My family has been good Christians for many generations."

"Good Christians? That's what the Puritans said, too, right before they set up the nooses."

"Dammit Tessa, stop it. We are not our ancestors. Why would you have the right to condemn me, any more than I you?"

"Me?"

"Yes you. You're a Wiccan—you practice witchcraft, right?"

"What are you getting at?"

"I'm getting at personal choice. Were you planning to cast a spell on me? Try to take my free will away?"

"No, I told you I wasn't."

"Then why would you assume I would sit in judgment of you?" His voice softened a little as he dropped the book on the bed and stood up facing her.

"Sarah said—"

"I am a descendent, that's all I am, just like you are to Sarah. Do you hold her personal beliefs?"

"I don't know what her beliefs were."

"Did you know she was described as an insane woman, harsh and abusive with her children, begging door to door and then lashing out at those who turned her away?"

"The history books said a lot of things; it doesn't mean any of them were true."

"Fair enough, but why do you assume they aren't true? Why do you assume I share John Hawthorn's beliefs?"

"I—I—don't know."

"Look, this whole thing got blown out of proportion. Why did you come here tonight?"

"You know why—"

"Just indulge me here."

"To be close to someone—you."

"Right, and that was my purpose, too. Why does the rambling of a ghost at a séance have anything to do with this?" He moved close to her and caressed her shaking arms.

"I'm—confused."

"You have your faith, I have mine, and neither denotes harming others, does it?"

"No."

"Then let's leave the past where it belongs—in the past."

Standing silent, she stared into the depths of his chocolate brown eyes. She saw no hint of deception—just sincerity.

"I don't know what's wrong with me." Tears collected at her stinging rims again.

"I do."

"What?"

"It's this Godforsaken book, Tessa. It has a negativity that affects people with distrust and superstition." He pointed to the bed where the ancient text lay. "Believe me, I know this book. I read it in seminary."

"What should I do? I haven't finished my thesis."

"That's what's important to you?"

"Yes—yes it is."

"Why?"

"I need to understand the past in order to prevent anything like this ever happening again. When I teach religions, I need to know everything to be effective, to be a good teacher."

"Oh my Lord, the secret to preventing this history from repeating itself doesn't lie in that horrific gibberish."

"You don't think so?"

"No, I don't. The secret is our faith, not only having it, but also teaching it to others. The atrocious things that happened were based on ignorance and primordial beliefs. We have an opportunity our ancestors never had."

"What's that?" Sniffing back her tears, Tess watched him from under a suffocating blanket of sadness.

"Not only to learn from the past, but to shape the future of others in their beliefs, educate them, teach them about the ultimate universal law." Brushing a strand of hair back from her face, he ran the warmth of his palm down her cheek.

"And it harm none, do what thou will."

"Exactly. Every faith has some foundation of good intentions and not harming."

"What about the old eye for an eye, Samson? That's a Christian belief."

"Actually, it's not. It's a primitive belief based on anger and revenge. Neither of those are the Christian way."

"Sounds like you know a thing or two about my thesis after all."

"It does?" His charismatic smile surfaced.

"I think so, as long as you can give me assurance on one thing."

"What's that?"

"That you agree men don't have superiority over women." She wiped her damp cheeks.

"I believe—"

"Go on." She stared him down.

"I believe that women, are in fact, superior to men."

"You do?"

"In many ways, yes."

"Are you saying that to get some, Mr. Langley?"

"Most definitely not." His chin raised a little as he watched her.

"Okay, then, I'll just be on my way." Inching backward, she eyed him with furrowed brows.

"What?"

"Just testing your point. Seems like you believe I hold all the cards, huh?"

"You know, Ms. Ledger, I think we're better suited for each other than we ever expected from 1Night Stand."

"Why's that?" Stepping a little closer to him, she could feel the heat of his body through her cotton sweater.

"Aside from the attraction—which I assume is mutual—?" He raised his brows and slid his arms around her waist, consuming her with his hungry stare.

"I suppose you could say that." She gave a sly grin, easing her arms around his neck.

"Even though we are of different faiths, we are both leaders in religion. I lead in church, and you lead—?"

"At Salem State University." She giggled.

"Ah, a university professor."

"I hadn't thought of it that way—the leadership thing."

"So I have one more question for you, Ms. Ledger."

"What's that?" She studied his succulent lips.

"Can we leave this religious business aside for now, and get on with the rest of the evening? Or are you done with our date now?" Loosening his grip on her waist, he pulled back a little with a teasing smile.

"Hmm, I don't think we have much of a choice now."

"Oh? Why not?" He pulled her to his chest and leaned in close, almost lip-to-lip, but not quite touching.

"Ah, it would appear that I have in fact bewitched you, dear sir."

"It does?" Giving a seductive smile, he pulled her tight against his chest.

"Apparently so." Sliding one hand down the length of his body, she gripped his semi-hard cock with tightened fingers.

"You have indeed, dear lady." He cupped his palm over hers, kneading her fingers along the shape of his growing hard on.

"Hold that thought." Tessa suddenly reeled back.

"What is it?"

"Gimme a minute." She rushed to the bathroom, collecting her candles and incense. She placed the items around the room, lighting them, and glanced back at him with a taunting smile. The glowing candlelight and the sweet, woody scent of patchouli brought a shudder of excitement through her chest and her core.

Finally, she turned off the overhead lights, glanced back at her waiting conquest, and found his stunning smile lighting up his handsome face. Samson removed the priest costume, dropping everything on the floor with a seductive glare.

"One more minute." She held up a trembling finger, grabbed another few items from her bag, raced to the bathroom, and shoved the door shut.

This is it, okay, sweetheart, damnation or desire? You are about to fuck a man of the church. She contemplated while she looked hard at her disheveled reflection. *Desire, without a doubt, desire.*

After a quick cleanup of her smudged make up, she pulled off her clothes and slipped into a snakeskin printed stretch mesh teddy. Stepping back from the mirror, she inspected the thong and the strappy criss-cross on the front and back. This was most definitely her favorite choice for risking damnation, sassy and sexy. Giving the final touch, a spritz of alluring ambrosia, she was primed for sin. Tessa's stomach was doing back flips with expectancy and the uncontrollable clatter of her teeth and internal trembles were too much to bear.

When she opened the door, she shut off the bathroom light and found Samson waiting in the bed, with the covers pulled down. Time to play.

Chapter Nine

The flow of her brilliant red, wavy locks and her slow saunter from the bathroom to the bed was exotic, and the wait for her arrival, unbearable. Samson had been with women before, but those he had dated were more reserved and never dressed like *this*. She knew how to work the moment from every movement of her hips to her fingers gripping the blankets as she ascended the mattress as full of temptation as Eve to Adam. Samson lay on his back, revealing his now upright erection. A sudden ripple of anticipation rolled over his chest.

Tessa climbed on top of him and straddled his thighs, leaving his steely hard on towering in front of her. She grasped it, caressing and rubbing from the throbbing shaft, up to the aching head.

"So Mr. Langley, you've never been with a witch before, have you?" Giving a deep, sultry whisper, she gripped a little tighter.

"No, I can't say that I have." Thrusting his pelvis as she massaged his manhood, he let out a low moan of pleasure.

"In that case, it's time for your initiation." His temptress reached over to the nightstand, took the burning votive candle, and held it over his cock.

"Whoa, whoa, what are you gonna do with that?" He struggled up on his elbows while his pulse raced with fear.

Grinning from ear to ear, she tilted the candle as the heated wax collected at the rim. The thought of the scorching wax on his dick was not arousing at all.

"Aw, is the big bad pastor afraid of a little hot wax on his nipples or the tip of his—" Samson flinched and squinted his eyes shut while he turned his head to the side, holding his breath and braced for torture.

A taunting giggle slipped out, but he didn't feel anything. He looked to find she couldn't contain herself anymore and she blew the candle out.

"What?" He patted down his chest and his vulnerable body parts.

"Just joking. I'm not into S&M." She laughed as his jaw fell open.

"Oh, that's it for you." He grabbed her waist, hiked her light but curvy body off his hips, and tossed her onto the bed on her back. Climbing on top her, he held her slender wrists above her head, grinning as she struggled to get away. "I'm gonna—" Samson paused in mid-sentence and the sudden shock of remorse washed over him as he loosened his hold.

"What is it?"

"I don't know what's come over me. I have never behaved like this."

"You're not hurting me, Samson, it's okay." Tessa reached up and pulled his face down to hers. "Damnation comes with a price."

"It does?"

"Yes." She chuckled. "It's called pleasure."

The corners of his mouth pulled back and eagerness rushed through him. The fullness of her luscious lips was irresistible. He leaned down; giving a soft and gentle kiss and then the intensity grew as she accepted his tongue. The urge for tenderness was overtaken by sheer lust and gluttony as he tugged her form-fitting teddy down her shoulders and eased it off her hips and her legs, flinging it behind him with a reckless abandon.

The deep, passionate kiss became engulfing; he felt as though he was absorbing her essence into his very cells. With a long, provocative lingering kiss, Samson eased his torso between her legs.

"Tell me what you want, Tess." He suckled her neck and throat, eager to please her.

"I want all of you, Samson." She reached down to his hips and urged him to move upward.

"Tell me, say what you want."

"I want to taste you. I want to suck your cock." She continued to pull him closer.

An intense, tickling sensation consumed his chest at her audacious words, and he loved it. He rose to his knees and inched up, kneeling over her, above her chest. The alluring redhead gripped his tingling hard on with both hands and took the tip of his head between her lips. The heat of her wet tongue made his legs go weak. He moaned, leaned forward, and slowly inched his rock hard flesh between her lips, gripping the headboard to steady himself as she sucked and licked, with long, slow, deep mouthfuls of his engorged cock.

"Wow, that feels amazing." He pivoted his pelvis and she took him so deep, his sensitive head rubbed against the back of her throat. Her hands slid to the flesh of his ass and pulled him in and out with compelling enthusiasm. Accepting him deeper and deeper into the length of her throat, she dug her nails into his stinging flesh.

"I don't want to come too fast."

Easing him out of her mouth, she veered up with a smirk. "Oh, you won't, I have plans for you, dear sir. Get up," she demanded. Samson stood at the edge of the bed, awaiting her next command.

She rolled over on her belly and glanced back over her shoulder at him, sending a silent message.

"Yes ma'am." He pushed a pillow under her tummy, raising her off the bed and massaged her hot, slippery wetness with his fingers.

"You like that, huh?"

"I love it." She arched against his hand as he buried his finger inside her. He ran his tongue along her pink, swollen folds. Her hot wetness spurred him on, and he wanted more. He lapped up her juices as he massaged her clit in tight circles, triggering little jerks of her thighs when he toyed with her mound.

"You taste so sweet." His choppy words came through emerging gasps, and he descended on her heated, fleshy folds again. Reaching under her, he grasped her breast then pinched and twisted her nipple between his fingers as he continued to plunge his tongue deep inside her.

"Take me now. I want you inside of me," she pleaded with shuddering breaths.

He pulled her to him and rubbed his aching shaft along her thigh.

"You do, huh?"

"Fuck me, Samson. Fuck me, now."

Samson reached over to the nightstand for the condom he put there when Tess was changing. He tore the flimsy package with his teeth and sheathed himself in a rush.

Rubbing his thick hardness along her dripping wet pussy, he eased the folds apart with his cock.

"This is what you want?" His fiery seductress wriggled against his shaft, incoherent cries falling from her lips. Easing into her, he buried his cock deep inside her.

A cry of pleasure erupted from her throat. "Ah yeah, you're so hard. Give it to me, hard."

This time, he entered her in one complete, slamming thrust.

"That's it, oh God, yes."

Relentless now, he impaled her, gripping her waist tight, plunging and pumping with a primal rhythm. She accepted him, squirming against him with every thrust and arching upward to take all of him.

He had surpassed his ability to maintain any self-control now. An aggressive wave rushed over him prompting him to fuck her hard, fast, and deep, obeying her every command. His primitive instinct had consumed him, shutting out any sense of right or savory behavior. Being so deep inside her hot, wet pussy sent rolling waves of spasms through his cock and into his balls.

"Tessa, I want to see your face." He pulled out and she sat up on her knees, looking back over her shoulder at him.

"Turn over and lie down for me, I want to see you, I want to kiss you."

She rolled to her back, and he swathed her body with his, plunging deep inside again. Tessa ran her tongue along the outline of his lips, evoking a growl of excitement. He pounded deeper and harder. Their tongues danced and curled around each other, with voracious suckling and kissing as their bodies rocked back and forth in perfect sync.

She ran her sharp nails the length of his tensed back as he surged inside her. She gripped his ass, pinching and digging her nails into his taut flesh, arching her back and pulling at his ass. With a whimper, she lifted her trembling pelvis up from the mattress, opening herself, and he penetrated even deeper. "Samson, oh yes, fuck me hard."

"Ah, Tessa, I'm gonna come." His frantic fingers rubbed and flicked her swollen nub as he plunged deeper and faster.

"Ah, come with me." His hand the only barrier between their hips, he stroked her clit to the brink of explosion.

"Yes, yes, I'm so close. Don't stop, harder, harder, ah yeah. Oh, that feels so good, keep rubbing my clit." She raised her body up to meet each slamming thrust. He could feel her muscles starting to tighten around his pulsating shaft. She arched against him, and they collided in perfect rhythm.

Tessa screamed as and her entire body stiffened. The pressure around his cock brought a growing spasm shooting through his body.

"Ah, that's it baby, I feel you coming, ah, you're so tight, ah, yes—"

Her body shuttered and clenched pushing him to the brink of explosion.

"Ah Tessa, I'm coming, I'm coming." The shooting spasm consumed his entire body, and the sting of her nails digging into his back magnified the intensity.

Chapter Ten

*H*is urgent gasps sped up, and his body stiffened in release as he let out a cry of deliverance and convulsed against her. Samson jerked violently, shuddering and groaning through his completion. In slowing, subtle, circular motions of his hips, he pressed deep embedding himself inside her. She whimpered in blissful agony, pushing up to meet his final plunges.

One last time, while impaling her with a deep constant push, he reclaimed her mouth. "That was incredible." He collapsed on top of her. Their shaking arms embraced each other tight as the blissful spasms rolled over her body.

A loud knock at the door startled Tessa.

"Well, I guess it's too late for the universe to interfere now." She laughed.

"No, in fact, it's perfect timing."

"What do you mean?" She sat up, pulling the sheet up to her chest. Getting up in a rush, he put on a robe and walked toward the door. He stopped and turned around, looking at her with a knowing grin.

"Did you complete your research tonight?"

"What?"

Samson opened the door to a young, bellhop in full uniform.

"You called for assistance, sir?"

"Yes, one minute please." He went over to the armchair in the corner of the room, collected a bundle of towels, and handed them to the bellhop along with a tip.

"Please have this burned—immediately."

"Burned? What?" Tessa gasped. Clutching the sheet, she pulled it around her body and jumped out of bed to investigate the mysterious package. She tore open the crude wrapping to find her book, the Malleus Maleficarum.

"What are you doing?"

"You heard Sarah, didn't you?" He glowered at her then offered a grin.

"When did you—?"

"When you were—ah—freshening up, you wouldn't want to disobey Sarah would you?" Samson trailed a finger down the length of her bare arm. Tessa paused for a moment, watching his face before replying.

"Make sure you douse it with lighter fluid and that nothing is left but ashes." She nodded to the confused lad.

"That's my girl." He gave a wink and closed the door despite the gaping jaw of the young man holding the unholy bundle.

"Now, where were we?" Strolling over he stared her down with hungry eyes.

"As luck would have it, we were just getting warmed up." She dropped the sheet to the floor.

"Oh?" He opened his robe and draped it over the chair, ready for another chance to please his fiery redhead.

"I did promise myself no holds barred tonight. I said I would do everything with you sexually."

"You did, huh?" He wrapped his arms around her waist, and then gave a slow, lingering, kiss, feeding from the sweetness of her lips.

"Let's see, you seem to have gotten over the whole man of the church thing tonight, we got over the deal with the book, what's your view on sodomy, handcuffs, and whips?"

Samson's eyes grew wide and his mouth dropped open.

"What?"

"I'm just kidding."

"You are?"

"Yes." She grabbed his hand and led him to the shower. "Yeah, I forgot to bring the whip. Maybe next time—for now, I can make do."

DESIGNING PASSION

BY

KALI WILLOWS

$\mathcal{R}$eading the questionnaire for the twentieth time, Tawny scanned her answers to the unbearably personal questions. With as much honesty as she could provide, filling out this page opened a can of worms she still might not be ready for.

Six years since she'd even accepted a date, let alone considered having a physical rendezvous with anyone, made the prospect of a match up with a complete stranger nerve wracking to say the least. Her pervasive physical desires—with a nudge from her friend, Laura—had forced their way through her cold exterior and frigid heart. Maybe a one-night stand would be enough to break the ice and give her a chance to move forward for the first time in years. After all, it was only sex. No commitment, no emotion, and no broken heart. One final attempt to experience the earth-shattering intensity she'd enjoyed with her first sexual encounter. Sex had become one disappointment after another; she'd almost given up altogether.

Tawny glared at her friend's email that had started it all.

Subject: Madame Evangeline.

Reading it again might remind her of why she agreed to seek 1NightStand's services.

Tawny, I know you've been hurt, but life is passing you by, and you're missing the best parts. I'm not suggesting you find love, but rather a chance to feel some joy for a change. Please consider contacting Madame Eve. Her reputation is solid, her service is legitimate, and she ensures the safety of all her clients. I promise it's confidential; no one will ever have to know. Do this

for you. Maybe, one day, you can at least smile again. I love you.
Laura.

With a resigned sigh, she closed the questionnaire and hit send, wincing as the outbox emptied in a flash. Done. She'd stalled for a week, obsessing over the questions that dredged up her painful past. Consumed in her black cloud moment, she jerked when the phone rang.

"Hello?"

"Hi, Tawny."

"Hey, Laura."

"Well?"

"Well what?" Tawny made no effort to curtail her irritation.

"Did you?"

She stared at the computer screen.

"Tawny?"

"*Yes.*" Drawing a deep breath, she prayed for patience. Laura meant well.

"Okay, I'm sorry, I didn't mean to sound so pushy."

She got up from her chair and walked to her fridge, thirsty. "I know, Laura. I'm—a little on edge."

"Was it hard to do?"

"I would rather have chewed glass and crawled over hot coals." She grabbed the orange juice, closed the door, and took a glass from the cupboard while cradling her lifeline between her ear and shoulder.

"Wow, so, better than you thought?" A soft chuckle slipped through the phone.

"Laura—" She stopped pouring.

"It's okay, Tawny, you did the right thing. Time to start living again, honey."

"So what now?"

"From what I understand, Madame Eve will review your profile and find an ideal match for you. You won't be disappointed."

"Huh! Can't disappoint someone who expects nothing." Carrying her drink, she plopped onto the kitchen stool and slumped over the island.

"Pessimist."

"Hey, I aim to please. There's no point in changing my attitude now, is there?"

"Anyway, once she finds a match, she'll contact you again and make the arrangements."

"I feel so pathetic, it's like—I'm desperate—paying someone to get me—"

"Listen, she's a classy lady with a high end matching service for the romantically impaired. You'll be fine."

"If you believe in her so much, why haven't you utilized her services? As I recall, you're not so *romantically* fit yourself these days."

"It just so happens, smartass, I sent my own questionnaire in an hour ago, thank you very much."

"Seriously?" Tawny couldn't believe her ears.

"Well, I figured if you can't beat 'em, join 'em." Her laughter gave her away; she shared Tawny's overwhelming nervousness. "Oh, I took the liberty of asking for a few special extras on your behalf. Okay, I have to leave for work now."

"Whoa, whoa, wait a minute. What do you mean a few extras? What the hell does that mean?" Fear raced through her heart as flashes of panicked imagination came flooding in, and she jerked her hand and had to grab for her wobbling juice glass.

"Oh, don't worry. I didn't suggest you wanted a threesome or bondage or anything. Relax."

"Relax? Are you kidding me?"

"I only suggested a little pampering and adventure might spice things up for you and take the edge off."

"Sweet Jesus, Laura, you're going to be the death of me."

"Will you let me know when you hear back from Madame Eve?"

"Of course I will. Talk to you later, troublemaker!"

"I love you too, Tawny."

Hanging up the phone, the uncommon feeling of the corners of her mouth pulling back into a grin stunned her. Tawny picked up her glass of juice and sat on the stool at the island, the heaviness of her heart lifting a little as she took a savoring sip of the tangy sweetness. There hadn't been a whole lot to smile about for a long time. She had become accustomed to being the eternal pessimist and overall wet blanket.

She could handle the concept of sex, but the possibility of caring for someone else brought a rush of grief crashing to the surface again. Her smile shrank back into quivering lips as waves of anguish washed over her chest. Would she ever be able to let go of him? Maybe Laura's idea had merit. A one-night stand didn't offer the same threat of loss and devastation. Going into an anonymous experience, solely for gratification had the potential to distract her from her torturous grief and emptiness. With a deep, cleansing breath, she turned off the monitor.

☘

Six different designs ran on his AutoCAD, multitasking second nature to him, when the sharp ringing of the phone pierced his concentration. A heavy groan escaped him as he reached for the cordless unit.

"Wyatt MacKenzie speaking."

"Hi, Wyatt, it's Jackson Castillo."

"Ah, my favorite client. How can I help you today?" Releasing a laugh, Wyatt pulled out his planner, saved his online work, and opened a new file.

"Wyatt, I got your email. The prelims you completed for the new site are exactly what we hoped for. We're looking to move to the next phase of development."

Pulling up the drafting for the project, Wyatt clicked and tapped away at the design while he spoke.

"Terrific. So have you decided on the style you want for the new site?"

"That's what we're still not clear on. I have a proposal for you, though."

"Oh? What would that be?"

"You've been a great architect and helped me put together some magnificent hotels for our chain. To put this project in perspective, I wonder if you would be willing to make a bit of a business trip for me."

"Where to, Jackson?" He stifled a chuckle. Jackson always kept him on his toes.

"I'm sending you an email. I'd like you to stay at one of the hotels we discussed modeling this next site after, but there is a catch. While you're gathering ideas that will fit the Rio locale, I have a personal matter for you to attend to as well. Take a look at the proposal, think it over, and get back to me."

"You're sounding mysterious, Jackson—what are you up to?" Wyatt's suspicions overtook his attempt at sounding aloof.

"The email will explain it all. We'll chat later. Let me know what you decide—I do have one request."

"What's that?"

"Try to keep an open mind."

"Jackson—"

"I'll talk to you later; the missus is meeting me in Gina's kitchen. We have some new dishes to sample. Bye."

Before he could respond, the phone went dead. Baffled and still suspicious, Wyatt opened his email. Dozens of messages downloaded and he scanned them until Jackson's address popped up.

The subject line had only a name: *Madame Evangeline.*

Clicking it open, he grabbed his mug and sipped at his steaming coffee. Halfway through taking a drink, he choked, spitting the hot brew on his open planner and the glowing monitor. "What the hell?"

Canvassing his desktop, he had nothing to clean up the mess. He jumped up, grabbed a box of Kleenex, wiped up the excess moisture, and sat down again.

Sopping up his chin and the front of his shirt, he strained to focus on the glaring words before him. "Matchmaking?" This had to be a joke. The most active playboy in America didn't need a matchmaking service. He turned spoiled debutantes away on a daily basis. There was no shortage of women in his life. Had Jackson lost his mind? Or was he playing a really bad joke?

Scrolling down, he read the explanation.

Wyatt, you're a hardworking man whom I have grown to respect a great deal. The women you see have proven themselves to be a disappointment. I thought, perhaps, I could offer you a small favor to repay you for everything you've done, helping me and my family with our hotel chain. Madame Eve is highly respected, private, and can make your wildest dreams come true—a one-night stand, with no gold diggers looking to land a bank account.

I realize you're a highly accomplished man in the romance department, but the way we have been keeping you so busy, traveling the world and building our hotels, has also cost you personally. No, this isn't a joke. Please think about it. If you're willing to be adventurous and give it a try, fill out her questionnaire and send it to her. She'll be in touch with you when she finds a good match. No commitment and no disappointment. Trust me; I know what I'm talking about.

Jackson

This was by far, the most absurd offer he'd ever received—a one-night stand through a dating service. Jackson did know how to get his goat. Challenging him to be adventurous always triggered a deep-rooted need to rise to the occasion. Cynically, he scoffed and opened the attachment as he began to gnaw on his lip.

The inside of his lip stung from the chewing when Wyatt sat back in disbelief and denial. *That pompous ass expects me to pour my heart and soul out to a faceless name on an email? For what, a night of sex? Sex I can get anywhere and anytime.*

Over the years, Wyatt had become quite a master at masking and even burying his feelings and his heartbreak. Now, he faced a personal interrogation, a page of seriously personal questions that opened up his vulnerabilities. The first question opened the door to the secret emotions he had avoided all this time.

Have you ever been in love?

Propelled by resentment and anger, he hammered away at the

keys, releasing years of pent-up frustration and sorrow. At first, he found it more of a cathartic device, to vent, rather than take it out on a valuable client who'd become a good friend. Jackson's intentions may have been ideal, but his actions....

An hour later, the very document that had sent him into a fury to begin with had become a project he wanted to finish. Completing the entire questionnaire had left him with a pressing sense of curiosity, rather than bitterness.

Maybe Jackson had a point. All the spoiled little rich girls who chased him had further soured his already broken sense of love and trust. The question that puzzled him most involved the level of passion he'd experienced. It asked about his most explosive and moving sexual encounter. He searched his mental catalogue of gratuitous memories. Hundreds of sexual conquests, all leaving some level of dissatisfaction. The most extreme and compelling experience he recalled occurred in his teens, with the girl who ripped his heart from his chest. She'd effectively ruined any chance for him to love again, let alone truly experience passion.

CB

Airports had never been her favorite places. Tawny glanced at her watch as she tapped her foot repeatedly.

"There you are! I've been looking all over for you." Sitting up with some relief, she glared at her tardy friend. "I've been going out of my mind. I thought you stood me up."

Laura dropped into the chair beside her, let her bags fall onto the floor, and exhaled.

"Oh, honey, I had trouble getting a cab, got stuck in traffic, but I'm here. Why would I stand you up?"

"I don't know, I thought maybe you weren't really having a— meeting—a—oh, you know what I mean." Her ears and cheeks flushed with heat as she tripped over her words.

"Oh, believe me Tawny, you are not the only one who needs some fun. You won't be going anywhere without me!"

"Flight 325 is now boarding at Gate 41," the overhead speaker boomed.

"Wow, I made it. Let's go."

"Uh—Laura?"

"Yeah?"

"Where exactly *are* we going?"

"I'm not sure. Madame Eve booked a private flight and didn't reveal the destination. Exciting, isn't it?"

"Exciting? Right." With a grumble, she stood up collecting her bags, and draped them over her slumped shoulder.

"Oh, lighten up, it's gonna be great."

They stepped into the surreal atmosphere of the small aircraft. The cabin's décor screamed royalty. Tawny and Laura took in the plush crimson seats, full bar at the back, and dimmed lighting. Classical music played softly in the background. The low hum and vibration of the engine provided an oddly soothing white noise. Tawny's stomach fluttered.

"We will be taking off shortly, ladies—can I tuck away your bags for you?" A charming, deep voice caught Tawny's attention. The handsome blond man at the end of the row held out his hands for their luggage. A second attendant, a stunning redhead, led them to their seats.

"May I offer you a glass of champagne to begin your vacation?" Her pleasant smile evoked a grin from Tawny.

"Yes, please."

"Honey, have you got anything stronger? I'm not much of a flyer," Laura chimed in.

Tawny gawked at her with raised brows. "Really? You're nervous?"

"Maybe, a little...okay, I'm shaking in my Jimmy Choos." Laura held up one foot and eased off the stylish stiletto.

"Well, that puts my worries at ease."

"Here you go, ladies. Look over our in-flight menu, and you have a selection of movies. Our flight will last five hours, so let's get you comfortable."

The pampering had begun. Surprisingly, Tawny began to enjoy herself—a little.

ભ

"Welcome to Calla del Castillo, Mr. MacKenzie." A familiar voice shook Wyatt from his awestruck daze. He spun around, following the sound.

"Jackson? You son of a gun, what the hell are you doing here?" Wyatt shook his head in disbelief as he eyed his dark-haired friend and paused a moment to admire the petite and extremely attractive blonde at his side. "Where exactly are we? No one would tell me anything on the plane. You know I'm not a big fan of surprises."

"Wyatt, my friend, life is too short to stay mad at your well-meaning comrade." He chuckled. "We are in La Savina, Formentera a small island off the coast of Spain. Remarkable, isn't it?" Jackson waved around the colossal foyer. "Let's get you checked into your suite and perhaps in an hour or so, you can join us for dinner and a drink. You must be tired and hungry after your long flight."

"I could use a hot shower and something to eat."

The concierge stepped forward, completing the check in. He handed Wyatt the room key card and a sealed manila envelope.

"What is this?"

"Your itinerary, sir."

"Itinerary?" A sigh of annoyance escaped before he could temper his response.

"No worries, dear friend. Tonight you can wind down and see the sights. Tomorrow...your journey to ecstasy will begin."

Wyatt eyed the poised man with exasperation at his lack of discretion and then caught the bashful expression worn by the attractive woman at his side. Her cheeks had grown bright red as she watched the floor, almost concealing her wide grin with dangling tendrils of flaxen—dear God, she knew what Jackson had planned. Wyatt was mortified.

On his walk toward the elevator, his design appraisal kicked in. Spanish Renaissance inspired décor featured handcrafted ornamental moldings around the gold framed doors. He admired endless rows of richly colored floor tiles laid in decorative patterns and deep, earthy tones of chestnut and mahogany brown that accentuated the Gothic-inspired furnishings of red strategically placed throughout the massive hall. The floor, the walls, the carvings, and the art highlighted the prestigious atmosphere. He approved.

In one swift motion, he flung his bags across the massive, king-sized bed. Rifling through his things, he mumbled under his breath. "Business before pleasure. I can't believe she knows what he's—" He stripped down on his way to the bathroom and stopped short of the doorway, marveling at the inviting steam shower with multi-directional massaging jets. Oh, this was a sacrifice he could force himself to make, for a "well-meaning comrade".

ԿՑ

The drive up the winding road revealed a hint of the breathtaking scenery.

"Oh my God, it's a castle, Tawny, and right on the water."

"Thanks for the play by play." Watching the view of the sea allowed her to avoid eye contact; hiding her fear had become a daunting task.

"Oh, stop being such a poop." Laura opened the window, letting the warm air flow through the back seat and across their faces. The ocean breeze teased strands from the confines of Tawny's hair clip.

As they pulled up to the front door, she admired the soothing, trickling of the cascading water fountain. She canvassed the magnificent array of colorful and fragrant flower beds, and nodded to two liveried porters.

"Good evening, ladies, and welcome to Casa del Castillo." The smiling older gentleman waiting by the entrance held out his hand to assist Tawny out of the car.

"Wow." Stunned, she followed her belongings on the porters' rolling rack into the hotel, unable to mask her astonishment at the glorious castle.

❧

"Well, Tawny, I guess this is it?"

"Separate suites—I thought we'd be in the same room." Unable to hide her frown, she burrowed through her purse for a tip.

"Well, duh, did you really think we would share a room for—the whole trip?"

"Ugh!"

"Okay, sorry you're touchy today."

"Ms. Reeve, we are ready to take you to your suite."

"Thank you." She followed the uniformed man, trying to hide the moisture spilling down her cheeks.

"Wait a minute," Laura commanded from behind her.

Tawny stopped, staring straight ahead, discreetly wiping away the wetness on the sleeve of her teal silk blouse.

"You forgot your itinerary, dear." Laura's smug tone irked her, and she held out her hand. She'd set it down on a table in her dismay.

"You're gonna have a great time, and so will I. Here's my room number. Call me when you get settled in; we can grab a bite to eat. My itinerary shows nothing scheduled tonight." Laura rubbed Tawny's shoulders with quick but tender hands.

"Fine." She walked briskly to the elevator still trying to hold back the rushing wave of frustration and sadness that overtook her chest.

❧

Tawny tipped the man and locked the door as he left. In an instant, she tore the camel envelope open and inspected the itinerary.

"Spa treatments? Hair salon? Esthetician? Costume shop...*masquerade ball?*"

The list overwhelmed her until she reached the nine p.m. time slot: *Meet your match under the rose covered chandelier at the ball. He will be holding a white orchid.*

Tawny had never experienced hyperventilation before, but her inability to catch her breath and fast-paced gasping clued her in. Clutching the envelope and papers in her hand, she rushed to the chaise and sat down, reaching for the phone. Her trembling fingers fumbled for the right numbers.

"Laura? Oh God, I can't do this."

೮૩

The tea had grown cold before she swallowed the last of the herbal brew.

"Are you any better now?"

Still somewhat slumped over, Tawny placed the cup down on the antique table and settled back into the posh, purple armchair.

"Yes, I know I'm a pain. I'm sorry; it became so real all of the sudden. Seeing the time and place and picturing...."

"Believe it or not, I had a similar reaction when I read mine. Mind you, I didn't almost pass out from lack of oxygen." Laura's light-hearted laughter was a welcome sound.

"I guess I did overreact, a little. Wait, you have the same itinerary?" A rush of hope flowed through her.

"Oh, no honey, I'm meeting my—date, *on the lanai at seven p.m .for a romantic dinner for two by the outdoor fireplace; wine, roses, and a night of earth-shattering sex.*" Laura's brows rose and a crinkle formed between them while her lips curled up at the sides.

"Uh, your list said earth-shattering sex?"

"No, of course not. It said *evening rendezvous.*" She clasped her hands together with fidgety fingers intertwining. "Okay, shall we order room service? Or brave the five-star restaurant downstairs? I hear they have an incredible lobster bisque."

"I can be ready in twenty minutes."

೮૩

Relaxing into the comfortable leather chair, she forced herself to remember how much she'd wanted to resist enjoying the extras Laura had requested for her. She hadn't planned on a makeover, but she sat at the mercy of a comb and a sweet, flamboyant Spanish stylist. The fact that Tawny willingly confided in him her reason for being on the island and the unusual circumstances of her date left her surprised at her candid honesty. Was it the relaxing sensation of his soothing fingers massaging the fragrant shampoo in her hair, or his sweet disposition and his enthusiasm at the details of her soon-to-be sordid interlude? Either way, she began to enjoy herself and unwind a little.

"Sweetheart, you have lovely hair, but we must tidy it up. We haven't been trimming nor treating it, have we? Oh, but I have an exquisite style for you. A little bit off here and there, some texture, frame your gorgeous face, and voila!" His expressive hands cradled and primped while he stood behind her demonstrating his creative vision.

She found it difficult to be annoyed with his enthusiasm, finding it touched a long buried part of her girlish soul. She'd avoided being the center of attention since her desolate teens. Her prolonged residency at the dreadful boarding school had taken care of any center stage tendencies she had a long time ago.

With hesitation, she winced at the mirror's image of him holding up lengths of her dark hair, clipping and trimming what seemed to be inches off. The wet, freshly cut strands hung, cradling her face and shoulders. Next, the loud, hot dryer, as he pulled and straightened her wavy locks. "You did a great job, Alejandro. Thank you." Tawny admired the sheen and the shapely cut. It hadn't occurred to her how straggly she had allowed her hair to become. Somehow, the new cut seemed to perk up her enthusiasm—a little.

"Oh darling, we aren't done quite yet, we'll arrange an elegant up-do to go with your masquerade costume."

"I haven't got a costume yet."

"Oh, but you do, and wait until you see yourself in it! Divine!"

His excitement compensated for her lack of eagerness for the time being.

"A little more luster, and, oh, perfection." Alejandro posed beside her in the mirror, admiring both their reflections.

"Now, my darling, off to Dulce for manicure, pedicure, oh and let's not forget the waxing—"

"*Waxing?*"

ভ

"Did you enjoy your brunch, my friend?" Jackson dabbed the corners of his mouth with the russet linen then flung it onto the table.

Settling back into his chair, Wyatt adjusted his pants button. "An incredible meal." Heaving a sigh, he looked up and stiffened then drew back. "Uh—excuse me, Leah; I almost forgot where I was."

"It's not a problem, Wyatt." The stunning blonde grinned and snuggled closer to her husband.

"Jackson, let's talk about the design you want for the Rio hotel. You want it similar to this—castle?"

"A remarkable concept, isn't it?" His dark eyes lit up as he leaned forward, speaking in a hushed voice.

"It's great, but the prelims were more—modern, I thought you said this was on the right track?"

"You're a high-concept designing genius; I know you can make it work. Some history, renaissance, exotic structure with more modern appeal to the vacationing population."

"Okay, but the site I scouted out in Rio had no structure in place. Are we building the hotel from scratch?"

"Actually Wyatt, that's the intriguing part. About twenty miles down the coastline you plotted out for me lies the remains of a 1715 fortress."

"Yes, I remember it. I drove down and explored the ruins."

"I had a feeling you would have. So you can envision the fortress before it fell to ruin?"

"Breathtaking, yes." Catching onto Jackson's train of thought, Wyatt grinned. "So just as this hotel is modeled after the ruins on the island, the Rio resort will take its inspiration from that structure.

"I knew you would understand." Giving an animated nod, he turned to Leah. "You see, darling, I told you, all I need is to start the vision, and Wyatt can bring it to life." A triumphant smile lit his face as he put his arm around his lady and squeezed her tight.

"I've emailed the pictures and specs, to you. Rebuilding the old structure in its resting place isn't feasible, but recreating the historic design, incorporated with your unique and extravagant construction plans, will make it the most revered hotel in the world."

Nodding and serious, Wyatt pulled out his planner and started jotting down a few things.

"You have inspiration now, right?" Jackson leaned toward him.

"Without a doubt." He continued writing.

"Then perhaps, my friend, you can tuck these ideas away for a night or two, do some more exploring of *this* castle and get further inspired." Jackson pulled at the still sealed envelope sticking out of Wyatt's planner.

"Oh, yeah, I—uh—yeah." Embarrassment returned as he shot a cautious glance at Leah.

"Have you read your itinerary yet?"

"Uh—no—"

"It's okay, she knows." Jackson's amused laughter filled the air, furthering Wyatt's horror.

"Oh, God." Hiding his humiliation in the palms of his hands, he shook his head in disbelief.

"Wyatt, please don't be embarrassed; it's nothing to be ashamed of." The tenderness of her sweet voice forced his gaze back to her. "That's actually how Jackson and I met."

"Oh? *Oh.*" Wyatt caught on.

"It's a long story, but Madame Eve knows her business."

"What does she have planned for you, Wyatt? Eve is surprisingly magical in her matchmaking abilities." Glancing at Jackson, Leah squeezed his hand.

"Well, I—we don't need to...."

"Oh, I didn't mean about the intimate part, but about the place you'll meet?"

With no dignity left to lose, Wyatt tore the envelope open. Examining the paper, he looked up, bewildered. "A masquerade?"

"Oh, yes!" Her sudden animation caught him by surprise. "We're hosting an extravagant gala tonight. Renaissance inspired. The ballroom will be bursting at the seams with masks and roses." Leah motioned with waving hands at the workers rolling carts of boxes into the back of the room. "We're having champagne and dancing, and it's a full moon tonight, expected to be a clear, cool evening where we can dance under the stars." Her dreamy expression revealed her starry-eyed aspirations for this event.

"Wyatt? You look so serious. Is there a problem?" Jackson queried.

Jaw tensing, Wyatt worked to appear devoid of emotion. "I don't understand. If this is just a one-night stand, why go through all the motions? Why so much build up for someone I'm never gonna see again."

"You're thinking too much. The idea is to have fun, a good time with no strings attached and no worries. We'll be there, in costume, if you need moral support." The robust chortle divulged Jackson's lack of sympathy to his distress.

"What my husband is trying to say—" Leah interceded, grabbing Jackson's hand and squeezing a little, "—is that the mystery of meeting a masked stranger for a discreet rendezvous could make things more interesting, don't you think? You work hard, Wyatt. A little fun, anonymity, a little adventure is a good thing."

Squirming in his seat under her dissecting gaze, he couldn't deny her point. She presented the same challenge, *adventure*. *Damn*.

"I guess you're right, Leah. I know I seem ungrateful, it's just, well—" He hated surrendering, "—where do I get a costume?" Sinking into his seat, he gave in to her.

"My understanding is that Eve has already taking care of everything for you. Let's go see my friend, Isabel, and get you all set up" Leah stood up, held out her hands for both men and escorted them out of the restaurant.

ೞ

The entrance to the ballroom was swathed with red roses and hung with an array of elegant masks. The foyer and ballroom glimmered with hundreds of candles. The air was perfumed with the fragrance of the blooms. The intoxicating aroma lifted her spirits and heightened her anticipation of what was about to transpire. Almost enough to distract Tawny from the exceptional panic that consumed her—almost.

Frozen on the spot, she stood at the entrance of the masquerade, unable to enter. Her shortness of breath returned. At first, she suspected her form-fitting corset provided the catalyst, but taking a quick inventory, she concluded its comfort level sufficient. No, the violent butterflies that wreaked havoc in her stomach had to be the culprits.

In another moment of doubt, she stepped backward as masked couples in costume passed by, entering the gala. Tawny scouted out the vast, bronzed mirror along the foyer wall, stepped in front of it, and stood in awe. The black and lavender gown with its magnificent layers of lavish purple materials and trims of black lace was quite extraordinary. The bodice accentuated the deep, squared neckline that cradled her breasts, showing more of them than she was completely comfortable revealing.

Okay Tawny, stop being such a coward. You can do this. With a deep exhale, she gathered her courage, secured her mauve and black lace mask to conceal her identity, and strolled into the ballroom.

Her shoes and costume were amazingly comfortable; the regal brocade dress weighty but luxurious. The jacquard silk chemise caressed her bare, silky-smooth thighs. She'd even discarded traditional pantyhose in favor of lavender garters that held sheer silken hose snugly in place.

"Senorita Reeve, please allow me to escort you." A gentleman held out his arm, waiting for her to accept. At the familiar voice, she

131

perused his powdered white wig and gold and fuchsia mask. A smile emerged when she realized his identity.

"Alejandro!" A sense of relief washed over her. He knew her secret, too, after her afternoon chatting in the comfort of his salon; she had already surpassed that embarrassment. Now she didn't feel completely alone. The journey to meeting her match came with yet another perk.

"Darling, look at you, I knew this costume and hairstyle would be exquisite. You look elegant, and sensual." His Spanish accent added to Tawny's enjoyment of his flattery.

"It's a good thing I'm wearing a mask, or you might see me blush, sir." A nervous giggle slipped out at the appearance of his mischievous grin.

The ballroom looked vast but charming. The pale yellow, flickering glow of the candles intensified the sheer enchantment of the evening. The cool, salty taste of the ocean air drifted into the room, drawing her attention to the open glass doors facing the sea.

"Would you like to see the lanai before the sun sets, Tawny?"

"The lanai?" Recollection of Laura's evening plans sparked her curiosity. Maybe she could catch a glimpse of them. To her dismay, she had forgotten to put on her watch, and scanned the room for a clock. Seeing none, she turned to her chaperone.

"Alejandro, what time is it?"

"It is eight forty-five; there are still a few minutes of light left." He ushered her across the room past the gathering congregation of masked revelers. The classical music in the background grew a little louder, muffling the chatter.

The cool breeze swept her loose curls across her neck as she stepped over the threshold to the lanai. A few clouds rolled by, parting and revealed the sunset at the edge of the waterline. In awe, Tawny walked to the concrete banister that led to spiraling stone steps off to the side. A glance across the sea bestowed the breathtaking vision of the endless azure waters brimming with the reddish-orange glow of the setting sun. The curling waves cascaded along the shore as she observed the sedate ambiance of the talc sand.

"I don't think I've ever seen anything so beautiful. If nothing else comes of tonight, at least this is a memory I can cherish." A feeling of serenity washed over her. Elicited by the view, the costume, the anonymity of the evening? Or was she actually starting to enjoy herself?

"Tawny, darling, it's almost time." The excitement in his voice brought the reality of the moment crashing to the surface again.

She glanced around for Laura, wishing for moral support. Tawny's eyes darted up and down the stone walkway to a small table for two placed near an outdoor fireplace.

In a panic, she raced to the shimmering light of the fire, only to find the table abandoned with drained wine glasses and half-eaten pasta the only sign of its recent occupancy. The tapered candles sputtered in the gentle wind. Laura had already gone, and the time to meet her date had come. A dash of nausea overwhelmed her for a moment.

"It's nearly nine, Ms. Reeve; will you join me in a toast?" Alejandro escorted her back through the door, stealing away two bubbling champagne flutes from a passing server.

"A toast?"

"Yes, to a remarkable evening and an exquisite lady." Placing the glass in her hand, he raised his, gently clinking them together.

The chocolate brown eyes that admired her through the mask evoked a shy smile as she dropped her chin a little, still catching his gaze. She took a sip of the sparkling drink. The delectable sweetness triggered an insatiable thirst, prompting her to sip, and then clumsily gulp, until the entire glass emptied.

"A connoisseur." He collected the crystal from her trembling hand. "You'll be fine, sweetheart." Alejandro faced her, primping her plunging neckline, and smoothing her dark tendrils to perfection. Tawny frowned at him. He cupped her cheeks with his palms. "I'll be standing by the door if you need me and believe me, you won't need me."

"Thank you." With a squeeze of his hand, she offered a beseeching gaze of gratitude before letting go.

Her eyes quested across the ceiling. There, in the middle of the dance floor, the rose covered chandelier dangled, beckoning her.

The crowed had grown thick. Wading through the vibrant and extravagant costumed couples heightened the pangs of anxiety rolling through her stomach and chest. Working to breathe slower, she stared up at the red roses as a few petals glided down around her.

I feel ridiculous. What if he sees me and leaves? The nagging voice in the back of her head drowned out the clatter of the room. Tawny glanced at the doorway, finding Alejandro watching her and nodding with a smile. Inhaling deeply, she pulled her shoulders back and her chin up, composing herself. A sudden tap on her shoulder startled her and she swung around.

A tall, striking man stood before her, clad in a black velvet, knee length coat and holding in his hand a single white orchid.

Tawny perused his luxuriant costume; he wore his chestnut brown hair slicked back into a ponytail. Thick, lush curls brushed his wide jacket collar and ivory ruffled shirt. A somewhat modernized version of the Venetian Colonial costume had the brocade vest and form-fitting, knee-length trousers with a codpiece, which drew her particular focus to how it accentuated his endowment. A spasm of longing rushed through her core as she watched the amber-green eyes fix on her from behind the obscuring black mask.

"I believe this is for you?" Offering the flower, he bowed in a debonair fashion, fitting of the attire he wore.

"Uh—thank you," she stuttered receiving the orchid. He collected her other hand and tenderly kissed the back of her fingers, his seductive gaze mesmerizing.

"You are—" Unsure of how to begin, she paused, shaking her head and huffing with embarrassment.

"A friend of Madame Eve's." He offered a grin with a raised brow.

"Yes, a friend." Relief stretched across her tense shoulders.

"Would you care to dance, my lady?" Holding out his hand, he watched her like a wolf to the sheep.

Apprehension flooded through her, but she fought her way

through the murky ambivalence. "I would be honored, sir." With a slight bow, she followed his lead, engaging in dance and moving swiftly, swirling and stepping in unison to the tempo of the lively baroque style melody. Getting lost in the music didn't take long, and the night of fantasy was underway.

From half an arm's length away, Tawny studied her companion's perfect, luscious lips, tanned skin, and striking features. His eyes astonished her; there was something familiar but captivating about them. The intense heat of his hand at her waist magnified through the majestic material, quickening her arousal. The grip of his hand over hers awakened the desire that had been dormant for so many years.

Part of Tawny wanted to skip the façade, the anticipation overwhelming. A curious glimpse down, revealed the most wonderful bulge, so tempting, so inviting, it was all she could do not to reach down and caress it.

Almost ready to succumb to him at first command, her knees grew weak when he pulled her closer; leaning in, he spoke in her ear. "Would you like to go for a walk and get to know each other?" His deep voice entranced her.

"Yes, I would." A shudder of excitement rolled over her.

He took her hand and led her out to the lanai. The clicking of her heels against the stone echoed down the spiraling steps. He didn't speak, his firm grip and fast pace becoming a turn on. Something about a stranger taking charge stirred her interest.

Browsing the landscape over the waist high stone wall, she observed the extraordinary glow of the clouds partially covering the full moon. The last glimmer of her perfect sunset began to fade into the water line.

"I was wandering the beach this morning; it's beautiful. There's a place I would like to see. Are you up for a little sex-ploration?" His smoldering eyes sent a slight spasm of excitement through her—if his gaze was enough to titillate her, oh what a night she was in for.

"All right."

At the foot of the staircase, Tawny stopped, removed her sparkling pumps, and carried them in her free hand. The cool grains of beach sand caressed her feet and buried her toes as she walked alongside him.

"What place?" Relishing the strength of his hand wrapped around hers, she stepped quickly to keep pace with his long legs.

"Down the beach is the tower and courtyard of the original castle this hotel was modeled after. It's quite beautiful if you would like to see it?"

"That sounds wonderful."

The thought of being out of sight of Alejandro brought about uneasiness, but she had developed a greater comfort level than she anticipated with her date. Her excitement grew.

Her weighty skirt flapped in the brisk wind, while the splashing sound of the heavy waves lapping against the sand and the rocks commanded her attention. A few stray seagulls walked solemnly along the waterline, scavenging through the swept up piles of sopping green seaweed. A flock of the squawking birds farther down the shore circled a larger prize, pulling and grabbing, then flew away with their bounty.

As an incoming wave of water and foam washed over Tawny's toes, the ebbing tide left a starfish sprawled helplessly in its wake.

"Oh, this is so beautiful." She gathered her skirt as she bent down to inspect the reddish, five-pointed creature. Her escort kneeled beside her.

"He's remarkable."

"How will it get back to the water?"

"That's the beauty of it; when something gets lost or misplaced, nature usually finds a way of getting it back to where it belongs." He gave a witty smile as the incoming whoosh of another wave drew closer. Taking her hand, he guided her to her feet before the cascading water arrived. Caught in his penetrating gaze, she followed his nod as he looked back to the wet sand left by the receding tide. To her pleasure, the starfish was gone.

"See, he's finding his way home as we speak."

Tawny returned his grin, still holding his hand. Off in the distance, the squawking of the seagulls faded as they flew away under the darkened sky. Her inhale carried the tangy odor of brine and the heady scent of musty ocean life.

They walked hand in hand while she eyed the shallow pools left in the hollows of the shoreline.

"Are you cold?" The mystery man paused, removing his long coat. Before she could reply, he draped it around her exposed shoulders.

"Thank you."

"I look forward to taking it off, too." He pulled the edges of the coat over her exposed flesh with a dark, sexy grin.

Tawny's pulse raced as a jolt rippled through her core forcing her to slow her breathing to a more deliberate pace. She hadn't expected to find her date quite so attractive. She hadn't even seen his face, but those eyes, those entrancing eyes....

"I'm not so good at—this. I've never, ever...." He shook his head from side to side.

"Neither have I," Tawny blurted out with relief, and the warmth of her cheeks grew against the chilly gusts.

"Would you mind terribly if I asked a personal question?"

"I suppose that would depend on the question."

"That's fair enough." He laughed. "You are a beautiful woman, maybe a little shy, but what made you—" His loss of words evoked an embarrassed laugh from her.

"What made me want a one-night stand?"

"Yeah." His nod and deep sigh revealed apprehension and anxiety that echoed her own.

"Honestly? My friend—uh—encouraged me."

The uneasy knots in her stomach began to restrict her breathing. She cleared her throat. Tawny hadn't expected any sharing of personal motives, but remarkably, she didn't mind admitting her hopes to him.

"I lost someone I loved a long time ago, and never got over it. Life has been—difficult. I guess my friend wanted me to try to move on, and this just seemed easier."

"I see." His gaze fell to the taupe grains coating her toes.

"And you?"

"I—a long time ago—I—" She found his flustered tone

endearing. Letting out a deep exhale, he continued in a more composed fashion. "I suppose I needed the same encouragement."

Their silence lingered until the wind began to gust. The whitecaps crashed against the shore with increasing intensity. A heavy cloud cover rolled in.

The howling wind brought the faded sound of rumbling thunder. Flashes of booming white light lit up the mass of clouds, followed by a louder crack as the storm approached.

The ominous air sent shivers down Tawny's spine. Her body tensed, watching the storm front amplify before her eyes. "Well, so much for a clear night with a full moon," she offered through clenched, chattering teeth.

"We should find some shelter." Concern filled his voice as he looked up to the flashing sky. "We're too far from the hotel to turn back now; we'll get caught in the storm."

Another flash lit up the sky, revealing a stone structure a short way down the beach. "The ruins; we may be able to stay dry in there." He took her hand and led her toward the faded magnificence of a crumbling castle tower. A crashing bolt of forked lightning struck a tree at the top of the cliff; forcing them to run as a drenching rain began.

Tawny clung to her date's hand as they raced through the torrential downpour and into the stone archway of the castle tower.

Panting with exhaustion, she wiped the cold wetness away from her face and smoothed down her saturated dress with trembling hands, pressing and ringing out the heavy material. The excess water dropped onto the hardened soil and stone slabs. The saturated coat over her shoulders seeped down her exposed breasts.

"I guess it didn't help much after all; let me get that for you." A soft laugh emerged as he collected it from her shoulders, dropping it on the ground.

"No, I suppose it didn't. It's dark in here." Face to face with her suitor, the heat of his breath on her face quickened her yearning as she eyed the silhouette of his chiseled face.

"I have a lighter." The glow of the dancing flame glistened on the moisture trickling down his face and dripping from his hair. He paused in front of her, inspecting her cleavage with ravenous eyes.

With the flickering lighter in one hand, the masked rogue brushed a strand of wet hair back from her cheek. Slowly, he trailed his fingers down her neck and along the outline of her dress. Tawny's eyes followed his fingers to find the fabric had altered with the wetness of the material. It now gripped tighter to her chest, augmenting her fleshy mounds. Her muscles shivered and tensed wherever his fingers drew near. The internal tremble resonated throughout her body at his single touch.

"Well I'll be damned."

"What?" She shuddered as he stepped away.

"It looks like we aren't the only ones who have been here to explore." Taking the light with him, he walked across the floor and clattered around.

"What is it?"

Another spark then a steady, bright glimmer.

"Candles, lots of candles." The mystery man lit wax tapers in iron candelabras soon illuminating the tower.

"Wow, this is rustic, but beautiful." Tawny walked around, inspecting the crumbling walls with her fingers, and eying the array of survival tools for their unexpected refuge.

"Unbelievable, there's a fireplace, too, and dry wood. It's like someone expected us to end up here—" His voice trailed off. "Jackson, you son of a..." He shook his head, grinning.

"Jackson?" Tawny joined him at the fireplace, shaking and chilled to the bone, watching as he stacked the pieces of wood into a tepee, pulling old papers from a box and crunching them up.

"A well-meaning friend." He snickered. "He knew I would explore this place. I have a thing for old ruins and—adventure."

"Oh." She moved closer to the building orange flame and rubbed her cold wet hands together, trying to warm up. Hiding the chatter of her teeth wasn't as easy as she had hoped.

"You must be frozen." He stood up, took her shaking hands into his, and chafed them briskly, creating warmth.

"Thank you."

Giving an appraising gaze, he reached for her mask. Tawny reeled back, holding it in place, avoiding his hands.

"I'm sorry—" she muttered when she caught the surprise in his expression.

"It's okay. I don't really want to show myself either. It's just, your eyes—I was tempted to look more closely. I can't explain it, but I'm feeling so drawn to you."

"I'm sorry, I'm not good at this, and it's been a long time for me." She stepped closer, looking up at his striking features.

"You're not going to believe this either." He grinned.

"What?"

"My friend left champagne and a few other treats." Motioning with one hand, he held her waist with the other, guiding her to the small table across the room. An old, weathered wood table sat covered with a red paisley cloth, a picnic basket, two champagne glasses, and a bottle sitting in ice bucket, chilling.

"Are you sure it was your friend?" She pulled the card from the basket.

Enjoy you two, compliments of Madame Evangeline.

Tawny peeked through the contents of the basket in amazement.

"Caviar, fresh strawberries, chocolate dip, wow, there's a whole feast here." Laura wasn't kidding when she said she'd requested a few extras. The pampering was exquisite. Her exhilaration soared, only matched by her accelerating arousal.

"Unbelievable."

She followed his gaze to discover a makeshift bed of several lavish blankets and pillows on the floor. On top of the pillow lay a box of *For Her Pleasure Condoms* and a variety pack of flavored, heating lubricant.

"I guess they expect we're going to—uh—follow through with the evening's itinerary?" He drew closer to her with one hand still holding her waist. She looked up to find his brooding eyes watching her.

"This is so strange; I don't even know your name." Her inhibitions still lingered, although dampened somewhat.

"I'm—"

"No!" She placed her hand over his taut lips. "It's easier if I don't know." Her heart raced, every atom of her body beginning to quiver from the wet, the chill, and the growing excitement. A shock wave of longing ran through her. "No expectations, no commitment—"

"—and no disappointment," he finished.

A mutual grin was followed by the sweetest silence. His invading eyes were intoxicating. The butterflies somersaulted in her stomach. The urge to kiss him consumed her; her chest grew tight with anticipation. She couldn't hold back any longer. She had to taste his lips.

Tawny inhaled deeply, gathering her courage. She placed her hands along the sides of his face, cradling his cheeks as she plotted her target. His reception made it easy for her to be the initiator. With a final exhale, she released the last of her modesty and leaned in, soliciting the first taste of his succulent mouth.

Although she initiated the kiss, she succumbed to his commanding lips. With obsessive force, he pulled her against the hardness of his body, but leaned his head back and examined her eyes.

"So stranger, are you up for a little adventure?" He peered down at her, taunting, moving closer to her and then pulling away when she tried to accept him.

"Are you?" She challenged with a seductive grin. Mirroring his tease, she held back as he moved in again. She leaned farther as he gripped her waist, urging her close and not letting go.

"You have no idea."

"Neither do you. It's been a long time for me, and I have a lot of catching up to do."

He clutched her hair while he pulled her to his fervent lips. Lost in the warm wetness of his kiss, she was surprised to discover her hands moving of their own accord, pulling open the cold, wet shirt, and exploring the hard plains of his chest and abdomen with her fingers. The heat of his skin and firmness of his sculpted muscles spurred her on to push the sopping clothes off his shoulders.

Accepting his tongue with hers, and his hands around her body, she welcomed the impatient removal of her dress and then her chemise.

While his roaming hands fondled the shape of her corset, her aching breasts spilled over the confines of her bodice. The exquisite heat of his mouth quested down her neck to her chest. She let out a sigh of bliss, and then a gasp when he captured the peak of her erect nipple in his teeth and sucked it into his warm mouth.

She tugged at his pants, pushing them off his hips and gripping the firm flesh of his ass as he stepped out of the restriction of his trousers. He reclaimed her lips, holding the back of her neck and pulling her closer. His tongue danced around hers, while he removed the rest of her garments, leaving her only in her mask.

His powerful hands stroked along the flesh of her inner thighs. His penetrating eyes bewitched her.

"I have something you want." Giving a devilishly sexy grin, his hand grasped hers, guiding it down his chest, along his abdomen, until it rested on his sinewy flesh.

"Oh, you certainly do." She gripped it eagerly, stroking its length and cupping the head, while she trailed her tongue along the shape of his succulent lips. His breathing sped up and a low groan built in the back of his throat and rolled out as her tongue swept the inside of his mouth, darting away at his reprisal. She stroked his hardness again, a little firmer, a little slower while she savored his moist kiss.

Tawny paused, leaned back, and observed his reaction when she brought her hand back up to her tongue and licked it leisurely, releasing wetness into her palm. With a seductive grin, she grabbed hold of his steely hard on, massaging it, the swelling vein along the shaft pulsating in her hand.

"Oh, I'm gonna make you squeal." He pulled her closer, devouring her mouth. After slowly breaking the kiss, he rifled through the basket with one hand, pulling out strawberries and chocolate. Eying the sweet temptations, her mouth watered at the sight of the plump fruit. *Chocolate and sex, it can't get any better than that.*

The crackling of the burning logs sputtered and misty swirls of musky smoke filled the air as they moved past the blasting heat of the fire, aiming for the blankets without once parting.

Her mystery man tossed the treats near the end of the pallet, and with a swift, but tender motion, he eased her onto the pile of blankets, positioning himself on top of her. Her anticipation amplified with the warmth of his chest pressing against her hardened nipples and the divine pleasure of his swiveling hips against hers. The light chafing of his rock hard cock against her flesh was sheer ecstasy.

"Do you want me?" He ran his tongue along the contours of her ear.

"Yes," she panted.

"So impatient," he teased, ravaging her neck, sucking and biting. "God, you're gorgeous. The taste of your kiss is so sweet. I can't wait to enjoy the rest of you." Gentle sweeps of his tongue over her quivering lips sent spasms through her wet folds.

His hands explored the lengths of her body as she dragged the tips of her nails along the plains of his muscular shoulders and back.

He eased her thighs apart with his fingers and massaged her wetness, evoking louder groans of euphoria from her. The bucketing rain grew deafening. Blinding light filled the tower, simultaneous with a crashing clap of thunder, which resonated throughout the stone and the ground beneath them.

Tawny's stomach fluttered with excitement when he propped himself up with his arms, and trailed a flurry of kisses down her neck and chest, sucking and biting. The wet locks of his trailing hair glided down her stomach, caressing her skin, leaving cooling moisture that sent shivers running over her.

"Oh I want a sweet snack." He dipped a big, juicy strawberry into the chocolate.

The heated trail of his lips paused where his gifted fingers massaged, pinched, and rubbed her clit. The other hand, he grazed the cold fruit over her fleshy folds.

The heat of his breath on her skin was followed by a gentle

wetness of him licking along her throbbing pussy. Tawny's back arched as she welcomed his hungry sampling. The electrifying sensation of his hot tongue sliding into her swollen mound sent spasms of delight throughout her core. Looking up at her, he bit into the red berry, sucking the fruit while he drove his finger inside of her, massaging her inner walls to elation. Tawny shuddered with bliss, wanting him desperately.

Giving an entrancing stare, he paused with a grin before burying his face between her legs again. Her engorged slit spasmed with his urgent sucking, flicking, and then gentle biting. The talented masked rogue brought her to the brink of explosion. The intensity of his tantalizing tongue massaging her throbbing flesh sent her reeling as she panted with delight. "Oh my God. I'm gonna come."

"Oh yeah, come for me. I wanna eat you out when you come." He slid his finger in, massaging the walls of her pussy as he suckled harder on her clit.

"Oh God, oh God—" She squealed and grunted as her body exploded with shooting spasms of sheer ecstasy. She jerked violently. Her heated wetness spilled out and he lapped up her juices hungrily.

Tawny guided his mouth back to hers. Tremors rolled over her quivering body, and she couldn't contain her husky rasps. She couldn't wait any longer; she wanted him now, more than she had wanted anyone in years. Probing down the plains of his sculpted abdomen, she grasped his thick shaft, massaging and stroking. "I bet I can make you come, too," she challenged.

"You're off to a good start." He held her hand over his cock, slowing the speed of her strokes and squeezing her fingers tighter.

Pushing his chest away with a firm hand, she eased him back up onto his knees and sat up. Tawny gave a seductive grin as he watched her. The sheer joy of having control drove her excitement higher. "You like to watch, don't you?"

"Yeah, I'd love to watch you suck my cock."

She tasted his hardness. His low moan prompted her to lick and then suck on the tip, empowered when his eyes closed and his head tilted back. Tawny took pleasure in savoring the engorged flesh, inducing untamed growls from him.

Mastering his cock, she cupped his balls in her left hand, and held her right at the base of his shaft, gripping tightly, taking pleasure at the sensation of his pulsing vein, and sucked and nibbled her way back to the tip. Moving her head in a slight rolling motion, she encircled the head repeatedly, consuming his length.

She was caught by surprise when he pulled away. His eyes dark with lust, he grabbed her shoulders and pinned her back onto the blankets. The sweetness of his breath brushed over her face as he hovered, gasping, far enough away that their lips could barely graze. His stare was penetrating as he tantalized her, rubbing his steely hard on against her dripping pussy, offering a smoldering grin.

Eager and frustrated, she pulled at his hips, welcoming him, but he resisted, still smiling through his black mask that glimmered in the candlelight. She was torn between her desire to see under his disguise and the opportunity to have all of him. With precision, he pivoted his torso, teasing her, moving closer, rubbing up and down the heat of her throbbing flesh. The confidence in his movement spurred her on, had her clawing at his back, begging for him without words.

"Do you want me?"

"Yes."

"Then say it." A teasing roll of his hips fueled her yearning as his hardness massaged her mound.

"I want you."

She writhed under his powerful body as he pleasured her with the scraping of his whiskers around her lips, inflaming the urgency in tasting his kiss; the heated aroma of his musky cologne enthralled her.

"Uh—I can't take it anymore." He sat up, pulling her shoulders toward him. "It's time to make you squeal."

Ready for this moment, her breathing quickened. She watched as he grabbed one of the condoms and sheathed himself. Putty in his hands, she succumbed to his strength. He spun her around, landing her on her hands and knees as he gripped her hips from behind. Her pulse raced, her heart pounded.

"Shit, you turn me on. Do you want me inside you? Do you?"

"Yes, I want you inside me, now."

"I'm gonna fuck you so hard."

In a swift movement, he plunged deep inside her tight wetness. Tawny's cries of ecstasy filled the tower as the storm flashed and boomed outside.

"Do you like that?"

"Yes, don't stop."

Increasing his tempo, he plunged deeper inside her, harder, faster, clutching her hips while driving with desperate force into her. Whimpering with delight, she pushed against him in blissful swaying motion. Happy to be dominated by him, Tawny held her ass in the air while he pounded her hard from behind. He gripped her shoulders, pushing them down as he pumped, and she shuddered with each slamming thrust.

His fingers trailed down her arms, gripping her wrists. "You like giving me control?"

"Yes." Her body was ablaze with rippling waves of glorious contractions.

"What do you want?"

"I want you to come inside me."

"Oh yeah, I'm gonna explode so deep inside you."

He impaled her willing body and she arched her back, tilting her pelvis as he slammed into her, sending a shockwave of ecstasy through her core. She came screaming out with bliss.

He continued driving even faster into her taut, swollen flesh. In one final climactic instant, his harsh growl of masculine satisfaction filled the air.

"Oh fuck, you're amazing." His pace slowed, with long, deep thrusts, shuddering as his hands gripped her wrists. Finally, he collapsed onto her.

Tawny quivered beneath him as residual tremors jerked through her body.

ଔ

The squawking of seagulls sounded closer. Tawny opened her eyes in surprise for a moment, until she realized where she was. The disheveled mound of blankets had been strewn over the floor, one thin satin cover draped lightly over her body. She strained her eyes against the growing light that beamed through fractured stained glass.

The empty champagne glasses and bottle sat on the table alongside the half-eaten strawberries and chocolate and the faint odor of candle smoke still lingered in the air.

A brief stretch of her limbs revealed the stiffness in her back and thighs. They had made love into the early morning light before she'd fallen asleep in his arms.

Tawny rolled over, patting down the empty blankets and pillow beside her. Her remarkable conquest had vanished. It hadn't occurred to her that one-night arrangement didn't speak to what would happen when morning would come. With a sigh, she curled up, hugging his pillow as waves of self-conscious inhibitions returned.

"Did you sleep well, darling?" a rough voice called from across the room.

Startled, Tawny sat up, clutching the pillow against her chest. "You're still here." She released a half relieved sigh.

"Yes, I am, but I'm not the one with the history of taking off without saying good-bye—Tawny."

"What? How did you know my n—"

"I know everything about you." Holding up a scrap of lavender and black lace, he glared at her with hatred shooting from his eyes.

Sometime while she slept, he had removed her disguise.

"What? How?" Tawny stood up, wrapping the blanket around her as panic surged through her. "How do you know me?"

Her intimate masked stranger got up from his chair and walked toward her, staring her down with a fierce look. Clad in last night's damp and disheveled costume, he approached her holding her lavender and lace attire in front of him with pursed lips. "How many guys have you dumped and crushed? You don't realize who I am?"

"I don't know what you're talking about; I don't even know your name."

Without a word, he watched her through the almond shaped slits of his mask. Welled up tears began collecting at the red rims of his eyes as he clenched his teeth. He threw her mask on the floor at her feet.

Tawny bent down, squatting as she worked to inhale through the pangs of fear. All strength had left her body. With a heavy hand, she reached to pick it up, and cringed when a second mask of black satin dropped beside her delicate disguise.

Tawny collected the mask looking at it with regret. Tears began to seep from her eyes as she sniffed back the dripping moisture from her nose. His musky scent lingered on it. She inhaled, savoring the last of any joy this adventure had left to offer. Salty wetness dribbled down over her trembling lips. She didn't want this. She didn't want to know anything about him. Now, the complications she feared had become reality. Gathering her strength, she rose to her feet, holding the two masks, avoiding his stare.

"Look at me, dammit. You owe me that much." His voice broke on the command.

Confused, she contemplated a witty response, but failed to summon the courage. She didn't want to see his face.

"Look at me." He roared and grabbed her arms and shook her abruptly. "I said look at me, Tawny."

Hesitant, she complied.

"Oh my God." She wheezed and stumbled backward clumsily. "But you're dead." Her eyes widened with horror as she backed away, clutching her blanket to her chest. Tawny's feet got caught up in the length of the satin material dragging on the floor behind her. She toppled over, striking her head. The sharp pain was overtaken with looming darkness.

03

Her head throbbed relentlessly. Unwilling to open her eyes, she lay still, gripping the down filled duvet, pulling it up to her aching chin. Focusing on her breathing, the muffled sound of voices in the distance alerted her. Laura, and—him. Arguing.

Not knowing what was happening; the sudden replay in her head of the events before this moment came flooding back. Waves of remorse and confusion rushed over her. "Why the hell would she do this?" His tone was loud enough to make her want to scream, the throbbing in her eyes increased in proportion to his volume.

"Wyatt, I'm telling you, she thought you died; she had no idea. She never left you." Loyal Laura, defending her as usual.

"Oh no? Then what about the letter she left me?"

"What letter?"

"A typed letter, in an envelope with my name on it. That's all that I found when I climbed up to her window that night."

Letter? Tawny searched her memory to no avail.

"I had my pickup truck packed and running. I did what we agreed on, I climbed the rose trellis. She broke my heart."

"Wyatt, her parents told her you died in a car crash. It devastated her. They put her in a boarding school and left her there while they jetted around the world. Tawny has been mourning you ever since."

"She really thought I died?" His tone softened with bewilderment.

"When she lost the love of her life, a part of her died that night."

"How do you know so much about it?"

"Tawny and I went to boarding school together for four years. She is my best friend."

"Boarding school? She always said she would never set foot in one. Her parents threatened to put her there; that's why we decided to elope."

"She never would have in a million years, but the moment she thought you were dead, she lost her will to live and had no fight left in her. She never recovered."

"Oh my God, I can't believe all this time...."

149

"What?"

"I thought she—I—"

"She never said anything about a letter. What did it say?"

"When I climbed up to her window, I found that envelope taped right to the glass. I took it and put it in my pocket and tried to open the window. The house was dark. Her room was empty. I sat in my truck reading this cold, impersonal note from her, telling me I would never be the man she deserved. It said I would never amount to anything, never be able to take care of her, and could never love her enough."

"Why would you think she wrote that letter? Did she sign it?"

"No, but it was typed on the old typewriter I got her at a swap meet. It had a missing *W*."

"Oh Wyatt, they didn't! I knew Bill and Deloris were cold, but I never imagined they would have done something like that."

"The night we decided to get married she assured me money would never sway her feelings for me. She promised to always love me and that we would find our way in the world together. She knew I had no family, nothing, except for her. When she left, it crushed me." His voice cracked.

Tawny stood in the doorway watching him as he fell into the chair, dropping his head into his hands. Laura patted his back trying to soothe him.

"Wyatt, I had no idea. I thought—" she choked, unable to say the words.

"I should have known. They said they would never let us be together. I should have doubted them. I should have—"

Tawny fell to her knees as she cried; her aching head pulsating from the pressure. The warmth of his hands on her arms brought some relief as he eased her to her feet. Wyatt took her into his embrace and held her tight while Tawny sobbed into his shoulder.

"Fifteen years, all this time, wasted."

"So you really did love me, Tawny?" He held her at arm's length, examining her eyes.

"Wyatt, I never stopped loving you."

"Wow."

"Starfish." She half laughed as she sobbed.

"Starfish?"

"Yesterday, on the beach, remember?" Tawny cupped his wet cheek in the palm of her hand.

"Yes, our starfish; looks like it wasn't the only one nature helped to find his way back to where it belonged."

A soft sound of sniveling beside them distracted Tawny from her moment of bitter-sweet glee. "Laura?"

Her friend wiped her own tears away. A knock broke the tender moment. "I'll get it." Laura jumped up and opened the door. "Yes, Doctor, please come in, she's awake."

As the doctor examined her, Tawny sat up on the bed, still dumbfounded and shocked. Wyatt sat at her side, holding her hand.

"Yes Ms. Reeve, it seems you have a minor concussion, the cut on your scalp from the fall doesn't need any stitches. You're very fortunate." He patted her arm, offering a professional, reassuring smile.

"I guess I am, now." She grinned, squeezing Wyatt's hand.

"I'll see you out, Doctor." Wyatt escorted the short, stout man to the door.

He opened it, and another man's voice rang out, hearty and loud. "Well, Wyatt, a night of romance, only you would end up with someone getting knocked out." He chortled.

"Funny Jackson." He spoke with a low grumble.

"May we?"

"Of course." Wyatt stepped aside welcoming a couple into the room.

"Jackson, Leah, I have someone I would like you to meet." He walked into the room and the handsome couple followed. "Tawny, this is my—well-meaning friend Jackson, and his lovely wife Leah." Wyatt's charming voice now filled with pride. "You guys won't believe this but Tawny—"

"Madame Evangeline has a remarkable gift, Wyatt, I trust you now agree?" Leah grinned with an impish light in her eyes.

"I suppose I do now." He laughed.

Tawny sighed. All these people, when she really just wanted to be alone with Wyatt, after all these years....

"Well, it seems it's getting crowded in here, perhaps you will all join us at our special table for brunch downstairs?" Jackson wrapped an arm around his wife and smiled.

"You guys go ahead." Tawny blushed a little. "We'll catch up with you." Gazing at Wyatt, she communicated a different type of appetite. Catching onto her thinking, he opened the door, escorting the cheerful crowd out, and locked the door behind them.

Terminal Lust

By

Kali Willows

Chapter One

Overwhelmed by excruciating panic, she worked to free her arms, legs, and heavy chest. Trying to force a scream out, nothing worked—her eyelids the only part of her paralyzed body that obeyed her.

Ambrosia squinted hard and forced herself to inhale a slow, deep breath, then tried to wiggle her fingers. The slight twitch empowered her. She moved her toes, and then her head a little, side to side, and finally she was gaining control. Drawing air in, the soothing whiff of amber and vanilla danced in her nose. The oil infuser at her bedside made waking up a little more enjoyable despite her discomfort.

Sighing with relief, she glanced over to the glaring red numbers on her nightstand. Three thirty-three. The same time every morning. This mundane existence was exhausting. Waking up with her heart pounding, perspiration streaming from every pore, despite the chill that overtook her body—was her illness taking its course? Restless now that her strength began to return, she flung the soaked covers off and eased her feet onto the cold floor, feeling around for her fuzzy slippers.

A cup of chamomile tea might help her get back to sleep and even warm up a little. Cloaking herself in her terrycloth housecoat, she wandered down to the kitchen, flicking lights on along her way. Ambrosia dragged the kettle to the tap and forced the faucet on with weak fingers. She curled up in her rocking chair by the window to read yesterday's paper.

She read over the local news, wishing she had some interest in anything outside of her self-pity. A carnival was in town this weekend—rides, games, derby. *A gypsy fortuneteller!* Her doctors could provide no explanation for her morning fright. Maybe the psychic could give her some answers. *I'll go tonight.*

The kettle clicked and Ambrosia hauled herself out of the chair. She gripped the handle with all her meager strength and poured the steaming water into her big cobalt mug. While the brew steeped, she wandered over to her desk and turned on her laptop. A number of emails downloaded, mostly spam, then she gasped—the reply she had been waiting for from Madame Evangeline. The date had been set.

෬

Bright, twinkling carnival lights had offered a thrill in her youth. The loud chatter of passersby, the continuous bantering of the carnies who tried to hustle unsuspecting parents into blowing a bundle on a tiny, fifty-cent stuffed bear, the buttery smell of popcorn and the hot sugar aroma of cotton candy....

Even the laughter of people at the games, and the screams of excitement on the clanking rollercoaster as it climbed to the terrifying top of the hill had no impact on her. She walked through the crowd on heavy legs, stepping over spilled pop containers, scattered midway tickets, and the rest of the trash that littered the asphalt. Connecting with nothing and no one, she was the equivalent of the walking dead.

Under the starlit sky, the primary colors of the striped tents loomed dark and dingy, perfect props for the eerie aura that encompassed the sultry summer evening. Ambrosia scanned the row of tents and then spotted the sign: *Madame Zovka's Fortune Telling.* Grabbing a handkerchief from her back pocket, she dabbed beads of perspiration from her forehead and temples as she approached the open flap.

"Come in child, I've been waiting for you."

An older gypsy woman with long, flowing silver hair sat behind a table in a black velvet and pink satin paisley shawl. Her gold-coined headscarf glittered in the flickering lights of the dozens of candles lit throughout the makeshift tent.

"Me?" Ambrosia eyed the woman patting the red tablecloth with her wrinkled hand.

"Yes, you dear, the one with questions about her sleep." The bright pink lipstick creased in dark lines over her weathered lips and the thick dusting of rouge on her wrinkled cheeks seemed fitting with her attire. Chantilly perfume, with the heady scent of sandalwood and orange blossoms lingered about her. A quaint and eccentric lady with kind blue eyes, and a smile that could melt an iceberg.

"How did you...?" Ambrosia's pulse began to race for the first time in weeks.

"Sit and have some tea, and we can have a nice chat, little one." Ambrosia nodded, easing her way into the squeaky, wooden folding chair.

"My name is Madame Zovka." She poured the tea from an old teapot.

"Hello, I'm Ambrosia."

"Your parents were romantics, weren't they dear, with a powerful draw to Greek and Roman times?"

"Yes." The question evoked a flash of warm, childhood memories of her beloved parents, reading her fascinating stories of the Greek gods. "I suppose that explains my unusual name."

"You still miss them so." Madame Zovka put the teapot down and patted her hand. "You were twelve when they passed?"

Ambrosia's stomach flipped. "Yes, in a car accident. Can you speak with them?" A tear started to form.

"My child, *you* speak to them all the time. They say you are such a sad person, but one of great strength and determination. Give me your hand, little one. Let me read your fortune." She put the teacup beside Ambrosia's left hand, collected her right one, and examined her palm.

"What do you see?" She was a little skeptical. Coming for a reading was probably pointless; she already knew her fate. It was undisputable.

"You have lost your faith; therefore you have lost your will, my dear." Madame traced her finger along the telling lines.

"It would seem so." The warmth of a tear spilled down her cheek. She didn't have the strength to hold it back.

"You stopped taking your medicine?" Madame glanced up with alarm in her eyes.

"Yes."

"They told you there is no hope. They gave you such a short time—six weeks?" She took in a sharp breath.

"Yes, I didn't see a need for pills and needles if there is no hope. I don't feel there's any dignity or quality of life for me in that."

"Your body has been through so much, it is understandable." Her grip tightened and the compassion in her expression was compelling.

"Was I wrong to do so?" A hint of hope sparked for a brief moment.

Madame looked down again, analyzing the map of her life and shook her head with a furrowed brows and pressed lips.

"I am sorry, child. I do not see healing for your illness; at least, not in the conventional way." She sat back, raised her teacup to her fuchsia stained lips, and sipped loudly.

Ambrosia's heart sank with defeat as the words saturated her soul—then struck a chord. "Wait, what do you mean conventional?"

"Your body is fragile and getting weaker every day. Your blood, your immune system cannot fight off the cancer any longer."

"That I knew." The slight animation dissolved. Why did she put herself through it—another false hope?

"It involves the taste of copper." The gypsy's brows rose along with her voice.

"Copper? What's that supposed to mean?"

"I can't see clearly, but there is an insatiable thirst."

"I don't get it." A sigh of frustration slipped out; her shoulders dropped.

"You have questions about awaking every morning at three thirty-three, and in such an uncomfortable way."

"Yes, why is that? Is it the leukemia? I can't move, I'm cold, but I sweat anyway, I'm panicked and it's always the exact same time when I wake up. Am I going crazy?"

"Not at all." She chortled.

"What's so funny?" Ambrosia's annoyance was rising.

"You have been busy in your sleep, seeking your true love."

"I have? I don't understand."

"Have you ever heard of astral projection?"

"Yes. It's like an out-of-body experience, right?" *Okay, where is she going with this?*

"Precisely. You have been traveling every night for months, seeking out your mate, your true love."

"Madame, you must be mistaken. I'm not in love...not even seeing anyone. I have no family, no friends. I don't dream at all anymore, much less travel in my sleep."

"That's not entirely true."

"I chose to be alone. The last bout of cancer hurt the people I was close to. I couldn't put anyone through it again, especially not this time—so I shut them all out."

"There is someone." The psychic stroked her hand and she shuddered, tugged at it, but the woman held firm. Any human contact threatened to awaken a connection to life she tried hard to sever.

"Oh?"

"You have found your match, but in your waking time you don't remember. You have had some very exciting rendezvous, my dear." Madame stared right through Ambrosia.

A slow fog rolled into the tent, chilling the air as it passed. It traveled across the ground and brushed over her sandaled feet. The coolness overtook Ambrosia's skin and she rubbed her bare arms, fighting off shivers. A cricket jumped onto the table and started chirping. Ambrosia motioned to shoo it away, but Madame Zovka waved her hands emphatically.

"No, no, leave it; this is a sign."

"A cricket is a sign?"

"Oh my dear, this is a very special message for you." She slurped her tea back and nodded at Ambrosia's cup. "Mind the leaves at the bottom; drink as much of the tea as you can."

Ambrosia's eyes widened in disbelief, but she gulped down the warm, spicy tea and held the chipped china cup out, waiting for more direction. The cricket's chirping grew loud and distracting; her eyes darted between the cup and the insect with annoyance.

"Now, make a wish and place your tea cup upside-down on the saucer. Let's see what your fortune is." Madame's voice was filled with excitement, a far cry from the doom and gloom she'd displayed a minute before.

"A wish?" *Huh! That's easy enough. I wish I wasn't about to die!* Ambrosia swirled the last of the tea over the loose leaves then carefully upended the cup.

When a second cricket appeared and jumped on Ambrosia's shoulder, the chirping grew even louder, this time, right in her ear. Then, it leapt next to the other one on the table, and the chirping stopped with a deafening silence.

"What just happened?" Ambrosia found it odd, but wasn't well versed in the habits of crickets.

"He was calling to her." Madame pointed to the new arrival. "Then *she* came to him."

"O—kay." *What else does she put in her tea? This woman is off her rocker.*

"Once they find each other, they become mates."

The happy pair hopped off the table and disappeared.

"Give me your cup." Madame motioned with her fingers.

Ambrosia pushed the saucer over. The old lady had most likely lost her marbles.

She lifted the cup and bent close to the leaves, studying the pattern. "He brings with him the promise of healing and true, eternal love."

"What? Who?"

"The one you see in your dreams every night. He calls and you go to him, freely. You are destined to be together forever." Her melting smile returned.

"Look, Madame Zovka, the tea was great and this was— interesting, but I think you missed the whole point." Heat filled her cheeks, as she chose her words with care. *The poor old dear means well, no reason to hurt her feelings.* "I have leukemia. I've been given six weeks to live." Admitting it aloud made it more real, immediate. "This whole *destiny, together forever* business is way off the mark and I can't—no—I *won't* get my hopes up. I have to be realistic."

"Child, you will meet, you will love, and you will live. A very different existence, but all the same, you will go on. There is one caution, however."

"Caution?"

"You have yet to learn *everything* about him."

"The man I don't know and don't remember—I have to learn more about him? Sure, that sounds about right." Her sarcasm choked her.

"Eternal love comes at a high price, dear." She reached for Ambrosia's hand and squeezed her fingers.

Ambrosia's eyes welled up and her chest ached with anger as she pulled her hand back.

"I'm paying the biggest price life has to give, and it comes with pain, loneliness and no promise of love. I'm all alone, and since I'm about to die, I find it hard to believe that's going to change at all." She flung some bills on the table and rose to leave. "I never should have come here."

"Wait, dear."

"No."

"I only ask one thing of you." Madame Zovka stood up, unhooked a cane from the back of her chair, and leaned on its support.

"What?" *How dare she ask anything of me?*

"I only request that you learn more about astral projection, how you can be aware while in that experience, and remember, it is important. Find a book and read it."

Ambrosia shot her a fiery glare with a torrent of tears streaming down her face, and then raced out of the tent.

About fifty feet back through the crowded midway, her legs grew weak and tired and she had to slow down or collapse. Fighting to catch her breath, she stumbled a little, lost her balance, and bumped into the back of a stranger with a clumsy thud.

"I beg your pardon, I didn't mean to...." She stopped. The tall man turned, his black T-shirt outlining a toned chest and muscular arms. Her lungs tightened as she struggled for oxygen—and fought her unexpected reaction.

"Are you all right?" His deep velvet voice shrouded her just before her knees gave out. Strong hands gripped her arms, easing her onto a bench at the side of the fairway.

"Thank you. I'm so embarrassed." Tears blurred her vision. Blinking them away, she found a striking man with shoulder-length, ebony hair, kneeling before her. He watched her with dark, smoldering eyes.

"I shouldn't have been in the way; I didn't realize there was a relay race going on tonight." His luscious lips curled back into a charming grin.

"My legs—just got away from me, I guess." Ambrosia ran her hands down her numb thighs, trying to force feeling back into them. The noise and clatter faded and she felt enveloped in a cloak of peace.

"You're very pale; should I get some help?" His eyes scanned her. "Are you hurt?"

"No, I'm fine, thank you." Self-conscious, she shifted her tank top into place and smoothed back her thinning hair.

"Are you sure?" He cupped icy fingers under her chin.

"Yes, thank you. Now that you mention it, you're a little pale yourself." Her teeth began to chatter.

"Well, you just about swept me off my feet." He grinned, evoking the flutter of manic butterflies in her stomach. The man oozed charisma.

"I should be on my way now." The dark pools of his eyes held a familiarity that drove her to search her mind. *Where have we met?*

"Do I know you?" She fisted her hands to keep from reaching for the sallow planes of his chiseled face.

"Well, I don't know. I'm new in town, so I haven't really had a chance to get out and meet anyone until tonight." His cool hands grasped hers as he spoke.

Feeling a little dazed by the smoothness of his voice and the touch of his skin, Ambrosia sighed softly.

"Oh—I see. Well, thank you for your assistance." She stared at his handsome face—pulled to him by some invisible, magnetic force.

"It was my pleasure."

"I've kept you long enough and it's getting late. I should go now." Ambrosia glanced down and her jaw dropped. The mysterious stranger took her thin wrist in his hand and inspected her wide silver bangle watch.

"Isn't that funny; your watch stopped at three thirty-three." He glanced at his arm and reset the time to eleven fifty-nine then wound her watch while he held her hand.

"There, that's better. I wouldn't want to have you go around thinking its three thirty-three when it's only midnight." His penetrating stare sent a shockwave of longing through her weakened body.

"Ah—once again, thank you, sir." She breathed in his warm, woodsy scent of lemon balsam and patchouli.

"My name is Desmond, Desmond Jacobs."

"I'm A—Ambrosia Thatcher."

"It's my pleasure to meet you, Ambrosia. What a beautiful name."

"Thank you—Desmond."

Ambrosia's muscles screamed as she got off the bench, and

she tucked her chin trying to hide the grimace of pain.

"I uh—I hope we can bump into each other again." The dark stranger stood as well, still facing her.

The corners of Ambrosia's mouth pulled up in response to his striking grin.

"Maybe, who knows?" She backed away with stumbling steps, finding it difficult to stop watching him. "Good night."

"Good night."

She worked her wobbly legs as quickly as she could and then turned around and walked away.

"Sweet dreams...." Ambrosia turned around to reply, but he was gone.

Chapter Two

She continued to experience the same paralyzed, terrified awakening at three thirty-three each morning. But now, she remembered the dreams—or whatever they were. Hovering, with no control over her body, floating under the chin of the Statue of Liberty. The cool breeze, the lapping waves below, police sirens in the distance...so real. She rubbed the very real bump on her head, incurred when she swung around, smacking into Lady Liberty's neck. A bizarre dream, and if that was astral projection, it was a lame attempt.

Ambrosia tried every technique she found in the esoteric tomes from her local bookstore in her futile attempts to astral project or even to remember if she had. When those failed, she turned to her old friend Google. The descriptions of relaxation and meditation methods were pointless. If she lay down or even sat to try the procedures, her sickness devoured her. Exhaustion overtook any vain attempts to relax. Usually she passed out, if not from fatigue then from the waves of agony that consumed her body.

Madame Zovka was a loon, and Ambrosia became furious that she'd believed her ridiculous tales. Sorting through her memories of that evening, her stomach fluttered at the sudden flash of dark, seductive eyes. An image of the stranger's devilishly sexy grin brought a smile to her face. Her watch had stopped at the exact time she woke every night—but why? It had worked perfectly since her run in that evening.

Desmond.

At the sudden shriek of the smoke alarm, she struggled into the kitchen. *I can't even feed myself anymore; this is ridiculous.* Infuriated tears streamed down her cheeks as she tossed the cindered toast into the sink.

◌

"The numbness is only going to get worse. I'm sorry, Ambrosia. You may have to consider using a wheelchair to get around." The doctor's sincere expression and gentle tone did nothing to ease her pain and anger.

"I'll walk until I have no use of my legs at all. I'm not using a damn wheelchair. I'm not an invalid."

"I realize how upsetting this is for you, but please, be realistic."

"Dr. Williams, I don't think I can stomach any more realism. I can't sleep through the night, I can barely eat or walk, and the pain is unbearable. Can't you just lie to me for a change?" She could hardly choke out the words as her throat grew thick. "Can't you at least offer a glimmer of hope or something I can cling to?" Unable to hold back the building sobs any longer, Ambrosia broke down.

She couldn't even muster the physical strength to climb down from the examination table. Her will just as strong and determined as ever, she cursed the battered body that lacked the ability to follow its direction.

"I would be giving you false hope. Your leukemia hasn't responded to any treatment, and your anemia has reached a critical stage." He slid her sleeve up her gangly forearm to reveal the excessive bruising that had now surfaced.

"If you would go back on your medicine, at least I could try to make you comfortable in your last—"

"In my last few weeks, right?"

"I'm afraid maybe days, if that. Your body is starting to shut down. Your pulse is weak, you've lost so much weight, your blood pressure is low, and your gross motor control is failing. Honestly, I should admit you to hospice care."

"No, I won't lie in a hospital bed, waiting to die."

"The leukemia is spreading faster than we expected." Standing at the sink, the doctor washed his hands. In a moment, he'd be in the hallway—and she'd be stranded on his damn table.

Working to slow her tearful sobs, Ambrosia hated that she had to beg for help. "Please help me down, Doctor. I have a date tonight and I have to get ready.

"A date?" His voice raised an octave, as he spun to stare at her in astonishment.

"My last date, so I'm gonna make it count." She accepted his hand and climbed down.

"Ambrosia."

"Mind over matter is my only recourse right now, so be it." Determined to defy his cynicism, she pulled out a prescription bottle and cranked it open. "Could you please get me some water?"

He filled a plastic cup at the sink and handed it to her. "You're taking your medicine?"

"Just the pain pills." She popped two tablets into her mouth and chased them with the tepid tap water. Tossing the empty cup into the wastebasket, she reached for her clothes. "Now if you'll excuse me, I need to get dressed and go prepare for my date."

"Ambrosia, you can't possibly...."

"Why not? I have secluded myself for months now. My family is all gone, but my friends looked at me with such pity, I couldn't bear it. I am taking this one night, with a complete stranger, to be held, to be cherished, to feel something for the last time. I'm not delusional, Dr. Williams. I'm lonely. This isn't a cure, but it is just what I need for tonight. Then maybe I can find some peace, can find the strength to face my own death."

"I see."

CR

The loneliness that consumed him for decades had taken its toll. He rarely left his loft, even to feed. Decorated in a Victorian style, his home had once been a welcome sanctuary, but melancholy had snuffed out pleasure even in his lovely surroundings. If this didn't work, he was going to go to sleep, and never wake up again—ever. A long-time, faithful friend had agreed to help him carry out his plan, but only if he first considered an alternative.

Contact Madame Evangeline and seek out another. Hunt for a distraction that would vanquish your misery for a night and give you a reason to reconsider your suicide mission.

He'd promised nothing, but since their discussion he'd made a discovery...one that had added a promise of light to his endless, dark existence. While traveling on the astral plane, he had encountered a woman. For months, he had enjoyed beautiful, erotic nights that gave him renewed interest in life—hope for a happy future.

Then, a few weeks before, she'd failed to appear, and he feared she never would again. He should have taken her when he had the chance. His appetite had been sharp, but his faith in eternal love had been so long repressed, he'd hesitated—and perhaps missed his only chance at happiness with her.

Once again hopeless, he contacted Madame Eve. His friend would not help him with his ultimate solution otherwise, but what was the point in finding another? His true mate had disappeared. He could only try to feed his insatiable sexual desires and perhaps find an inkling of tranquility.

Despite his ability to control his thirst for human blood, his sexual hunger had become debilitating, especially in the absence of his late night rendezvous with *her*. Closing his eyes, he tried to remember her delectable smell, the sweet taste of her kiss, the exquisite warmth of her body, but to no avail. The memories faded. He grabbed his cell phone and dialed.

"Aldon, it's Desmond."

"Hello, my dear friend."

"Have you had any success?" A brief attempt at sounding hopeful was fruitless.

"No, I was not able to locate her, it's as though she has completely vanished. I am sorry for letting you down."

"It isn't you who has let me down. I let myself down by holding back when I had her in my arms for the first time, the only time. I tracked her down, I found her and knew that was the moment, and I didn't take her." He sat.

"You were honorable in your self-control; you fought the instinct to turn her before she knew everything."

"Perhaps, but none of that matters now."

"Desmond, when was the last time you fed?"

"I am not sure, I haven't thought about it lately." He cast a guilty glance at the half-empty shelves of the glass-doored medical refrigerator across the room, untouched for weeks.

"Desmond, you have to feed before seeing a human for a night of—your bloodlust will overpower you."

"I have no appetite."

"I wish you would reconsider," His pleading words were offered with hushed voice.

"What will change in the next millennium that hasn't changed in the last? I have no interest in immortality, not anymore." Desmond grew tired of justifying his decision.

"You mean not without *her*?"

"It would seem so, my friend." Irritation was soon replaced with sadness.

"I can't believe it's happening tonight."

"That's why I'm calling. Having fulfilled your requirement, I am ready to complete our agreement, in the dawn's early light. I have reserved you a room in the Castillo Hotel, so there will be no need to delay."

"I don't think I can—"

"You can and you will." Determination colored his words. "You gave your word, and in all the time I have known you, you have never broken a promise. I'm counting on you."

"This isn't right." Aldon's voice grew louder.
"What's done is done; there is nothing left for me."
"As you wish, but I will miss you."
"Thank you."

Chapter Three

*S*tanding in the vast lobby of the hotel, Desmond reviewed Madame Evangeline's confirmation email once more.

As you have requested Mr. Jacobs, you have been booked into the Castillo Hotel and Resort on Peaks Island in Maine. All of your accommodations have been arranged.

Desmond put his phone away as he approached the concierge.

"Welcome, sir." The cheery older gentleman rambled on about the hotel's facilities, but Desmond was stuck in a dismal state with no eagerness about his evening plans, so the man's enthusiasm fell upon deaf ears.

Sliding the room card into the slot, he pushed the door open. The breathtaking view perked his mood up dramatically. In all his long life, he had never seen a sight quite like this. Perhaps he was completing an unintentional bucket list tonight.

Dropping his overcoat on the floor by the massive king-sized bed, he walked through the clear, tubular-shaped room. Neon blue surrounded him, with magnificent creatures swimming all around. The underwater hotel was a remarkable destination. This view of under-the-sea alone was enough to make his last night of existence worthwhile. Nose pressed to the glass, he examined the sponge-like coral reef and colorful vegetation outside the window, the small schools of vibrant fish swimming by.... So much life, yet the room and all it offered gave such peace and serenity.

Taking in the rest of the astounding suite, he grinned at the hot tub directly across from the bed. No need for privacy here. Watching the sea creatures in all their glory while soaking in the tub would be a joy for his date when she arrived; even if that was the only bliss he could offer a stranger tonight.

ভ

Covering her graying skin with makeup seemed to make her look even worse in the mirror. The more she worked at it, the less real she looked. Feeling useless in her vain attempt at sprucing herself up, she called the hotel salon and asked for someone to come up to her penthouse suite and give her a makeover.

The knock on the door brought a sense of relief and she walked with weak legs to answer it.

"Thank you for coming on such short notice." A petite brunette in a pink beautician's tunic nodded with a pleasant grin and strolled into the room, a large bag bristling with the tools of her trade slung over her shoulder.

"Hello Ms. Thatcher, my name is Pricilla." Approaching a small vanity by the window, she placed a white towel on the surface, and laid a daunting array of beauty supplies on the terry cloth. She tugged out the padded bench from under the table and Ambrosia sat, praying the woman could make her presentable.

"I can see where you were having difficulty; this makeup is much too dark for your creamy fair skin."

Pricilla was being kind with her choice of words. Ambrosia knew her complexion was comparable to a corpse now. With gentle hands, the beautician wiped the unflattering makeup off with soft sweeps of cool, moistened cotton pads.

"There now, a fresh start." Her bright eyes showed no shock or surprise as she pampered the sickly reflection that Ambrosia stared at in the mirror.

"I was trying to look a little more—healthy." Embarrassment

washed over her but was quickly gone as she watched the progress of her makeover.

"A little more bronze over these areas...there now, you look as though the sun has been kissing your skin."

"Wow, can I keep you with me everywhere I go?" Ambrosia eyed her reflection in amazement, and then it dawned on her how silly her comment was. This was likely the last makeup she would ever wear. She blinked the forming tears away. "Thank you, Pricilla; you've done an amazing job."

"Well, I think there are a few more things we can do to pamper you." She pulled out nail polish and emery boards.

ೞ

Taking a deep breath, Ambrosia tried to settle the insane butterflies wreaking havoc on her hollow stomach. Another dose of painkillers was helping, but not being able to eat made a mess of her already destroyed digestive system. Vertigo started to set in; the spinning imbalance sparked a wave of nausea and unease.

A rush of cold sweat started over her face and neck again, finally enveloping her entire body. She pulled her handkerchief from her purse and dabbed at the moisture, careful not to smudge her masterpiece of fake coloring.

When the door opened, she gasped in shock.

"You?"

"I can't believe it's you." Dark eyes entranced hers.

"We met at the—I bumped into you at the fair?" Ambrosia clutched her tight chest trying to inhale.

"Are you okay?" Desmond took her by the arms as her knees buckled.

"I'm having trouble—" She forced the air in and out as panic started to set in. Was she losing control of her lungs?

He assisted her to the bed and helped her to sit.

"Ambrosia, right?" His voice grew fainter.

"Yes." She tried to speak and everything faded to blackness.

"Thank you, Doctor. I will call down if anything changes." His deep velvet voice was followed by the clicking of a door closing. She opened her eyes.

"What happened? Where am I?" Her heart raced. Everything was blurry–she couldn't focus properly.

"Ambrosia, it's Desmond. You came to my room and passed out."

"Room three thirty three?"

"Yes, that's right. How are you feeling?" With a gentle motion, he smoothed her hair back from her face and caressed her cheek.

"I don't feel right, I can't move my legs, I can't see properly." Ambrosia's voice cracked.

"It's okay, I'm right here." Cold fingers wrapped around her hand.

"Desmond, there's something I need to tell you."

"I know."

"No, you don't, I shouldn't have come, and I thought I could handle it, Desmond I'm—"

"Hush now. I know everything. I'm right here; you don't ever have to be alone again." His cool fingers trailed along her neck.

"I'm dying."

"Don't say that."

"It's true. I had no business coming here tonight." She struggled to rise, frustrated and embarrassed that her weakness was so evident. Couldn't the universe spare her a little grace for one night?

"You don't remember, do you?" He slid his arm behind her back, supporting her as she sat up.

"Remember what? The fair?" She stiffened, pulling away

"Well, yes, that, too." He tucked her close to his side.

"What do you mean?"

"You don't recall anything else?"

"About what?"

"About me, about us. Ambrosia, don't you know me?"

"Should I?" She strained to see his face better. His features blurred, but so close, she could see more than just vague outlines.

"Three thirty-three," he whispered, his breath cool against her ear.

"What?"

"Three thirty-three has been our signal for months now."

"Signal?" Her cloudy brain began to clear—just a bit—and a flicker of light shone.

"Every night, we met, you and I. I always sent you back at three thirty-three, so you would make the connection when you awoke."

"I don't understand?"

The coolness of his palm cupped her cheek as she fought off another flash of cold sweat.

"My beloved Ambrosia, why can't you remember me? Everything we shared?"

"I don't—where did we meet?" A wave of frustration washed over her.

"In our dreams, my love. You are my soul mate."

Ambrosia's chest heaved and she grew lightheaded. All the strength in her body drained and she lost control of her muscles and slumped over. Just as her doctor predicted, everything in her body was shutting down.

"Three thirty—thr—"

"Hush now." He pulled her close and kissed her cheek, his arms wrapped tight around her.

"The gypsy told me, but I didn't believe her."

"What did she tell you?"

"That I went to you in my sleep, that we would love one another for eternity." The gypsy's words began to make sense—which worried her. "I thought she was crazy, why don't I know you?" Labored breathing evolved into wheezing.

"Your body is weak; it's using all its strength to function. Maybe you just didn't have enough energy left to remember."

"I wish I had longer. I wish I knew you—" The room faded to black.

Chapter Four

*H*e laid her gently back on the bed, her eyelids fluttering, but her limbs limp. Terror overrode his logic.

A sudden knock pulled him from stasis and he stumbled to open the door. *Aldon!* He dragged his mentor to the bed. *Tell me what to do.*

You have no other choice; you have to act now. Aldon's thoughts shot through Desmond's head.

It's wrong, she doesn't know yet. She doesn't even know who I am. I can't change her unless she can make her will known. He kept the conversation silent to avoid frightening her any more than she already was.

If you don't change her, she won't have any will left, she'll die. Aldon shot a fierce look at him.

From the end of the bed, he absorbed her sallow face, emaciated hands and arms. "She doesn't have long." Aldon's voice shattered the silence of the underwater room, and Desmond's heart jumped.

"If I change her without giving her a choice, she may hate me. You can't take back immortality."

"You can't give it if she's already dead, either."

"This isn't about me."

"It most certainly is." Aldon's emphatic tone shifted to a fierce growl. "Tonight, I expected to end the life of my friend—my son. Now there is a chance you can be happy and I won't have to endure this morbid deed. If you don't change her, I will, for your own sake." He moved from Desmond's side to stand beside the bed.

She lay with her head dropped to the side, her pulsing jugular exposed, and Desmond quailed at the purpose evident on Aldon's face, his looming posture as he bent close to Ambrosia leaving no doubt of his intent.

"No, you won't." Desmond's lips curled and his fangs extended. "Back away from her, right now."

"Then do it. Her pulse is slowing. Listen to her heart. It is going to stop any minute now."

He listened, and what he heard carried urgency, as though he was standing on the edge of a fifty-story building and about to jump, not as a vampire—but as a mortal who faced the end of his life.

The soft thumping began to fade.

"Now, Desmond, dammit, or so help me." Aldon leaned over her, brushing a few strands of limp hair away from her neck.

An overwhelming rush of fear and possessiveness erupted and Desmond shoved his maker aside. The agony of his breaking heart grew with every inch he drew closer to her throat. Either way, turning her or letting her die, he faced losing her again.

"What if I can't stop?" His voice shook. "I didn't feed, Aldon, the frenzy—"

"I will stop you if I have to. I swear it."

The thuds became sporadic and her chest heaved as she gasped for air.

"Now dammit, do it now," Aldon hissed.

Desmond knelt down beside her and kissed her forehead. The sweet scent of her skin had faded, but it was still intoxicating all the same. Pangs of thirst ran rampant through him and he tensed with bloodlust. He pushed away from her; his feeding instinct had been triggered. Fighting down the fear, he slid his arm behind her frail back and tugged her limp body across his lap, cradling her in his arms. With iron will, he clung to the last semblance of self-control he had to keep from ravaging her defenseless neck. Her chest had stopped moving, her heartbeat a faint vibration.

"Desmond, time's up."

The bitter venom began to seep from his fangs as he lowered his mouth to her tepid skin. After a second of hesitation, he gathered his courage and sank his teeth into her delectable flesh. The warmth of her blood spewing into his mouth sent a spasm of bliss through his body. His thirst took hold and he sucked harder, digging his fangs deeper into her lean tissue.

The sour flavor of cancer was only a minor distraction in his indulgence of her essence. This exquisite moment of creating an eternal bond with the woman of his dreams filled him with rapture.

"That's enough." Aldon's words barely registered, as his crazed hunger engulfed the last of his restraint.

Enough! Aldon's superior strength pulled him back as her warm juices spilled down his chin. "Pull yourself together. There isn't much time." Aldon held up one razor sharp nail-tipped finger. "Now, before it's too late."

Her blood was coursing through his veins, but his sense soon overtook Desmond's feeding delirium. He nodded and pulled back his shirtsleeve, exposing his wrist. Pain shot through his arm when Aldon sliced his flesh open, leaving a gaping wound. As his blood began to spill, he held his wrist over her mouth, letting the fluid drip onto her slightly parted, pale lips. He watched as the blood seeped into her mouth, but nothing happened. She didn't move, didn't flinch or respond.

"It's not working." Terror consumed him.

"Don't stop, just keep trying. Let the change happen."

Suddenly, Ambrosia's head shifted a little, her lips and mouth started to move. Her tongue eased out, slowly collecting the crimson liquid, and she began to moan. Her hands gripped his arm and pulled it closer to her open mouth. She drank his blood savagely. With her eyes still closed, she began to overpower

Desmond, savagely sucking his life.

After a few moments, Aldon reached over, placed a finger under her jaw, and pressed upward. Her head dropped, as she sank into unconsciousness again.

"Desmond, are you all right?"

"I—yes, I didn't expect her to take so much, so quickly."

Aldon patted his shoulder. "Are you weakened? Did she drain you?"

"No, it's not that."

"Then what?"

Desmond stared at her, lying in his arms, watching the change begin. "I've never turned anyone before." He held her tight, but his body went numb with shock.

"Yes, it is a most difficult task, one that comes with regret, relief, and much confusion. It will ease over time."

"We'll see when she awakes. It may not ease at all." Guilt washed over him as the taste of her blood lingered in his tingling mouth.

಄

For the first time in a long time, Ambrosia didn't awake paralyzed or fearful, she didn't feel cold, and she wasn't in pain. Was she dead? Was she astral projecting—she didn't remember trying this time.

The silky material pulled up to her chin was soft and luxurious. She stretched her stiff neck side to side then extended her arms over her head before she opened her eyes.

"You're awake." A deep voice reverberated, sending shimmers of bliss through her body.

"Desmond?"

"Yes, I'm here." She blinked, amazed to find him standing in front of a vivid aquatic display that filled the wall...all the walls...and the ceiling. "Are we under water?" Tossing the sheets away, Ambrosia went to his side and stared in amazed enchantment at the active display of marine life. "Has this been here all along?"

"Yes, but you were too sick to notice. I knew right away that was a bad sign." Desmond remained at the window, his profile like a stone statue.

"Ah—my stomach." She grimaced at the stabbing pains and leaned over, gripping her abdomen. "What happened?"

"You—you were ill. You're feeling better, I trust?" His voice seemed filled with unhappiness; maybe guilt? *But why?*

"Now that you mention it, I feel wonderful. I could run a marathon. I'm so hungry, so thirsty.... I haven't had an appetite for weeks." Amazed, she patted down her chest and legs, reveling in the surge of strength and wellness that streamed through her veins.

"I guess that medicine—"Ambrosia paused, scanning her memory. "I couldn't breathe, couldn't see—"A lingering copper-like flavor surprised her. "Did I eat something? I have a strange taste in my mouth."

"You—drank something." He held his hand over his wrist—bandaged—had it been injured before?

"Did I do something to hurt you? Did I have a seizure and bite you?" Her cheeks burned with humiliation at the thought. But the fresh, white gauze appeared brand new...what other explanation could there be. In her extremity, any kind of physical reaction was possible.

He continued to view their watery surroundings, but barked a short laugh at her comment. "Not exactly."

"Hold on, Desmond, everything is still fuzzy, can you please tell me what happened? Are you angry with me or something? Why won't you look at me?" She gripped his arm and his sleeve tore like paper.

"Oh—I'm sorry." Confusion grew as she looked at her hand. What she remembered as her sunken-in skin and boney fingers looked plump and healthy now.

"What the hell?" She patted her body down again, pausing at round, shapely breasts. She bolted to the bathroom, flicked on the light switch, and glared into the mirror in shock.

"What happened to me? I—was dying." She caressed her supple skin and examined her curvy figure and thick, long locks of strawberry blonde hair. Ambrosia stepped even closer to investigate the brilliance of her emerald eyes, that seemed to almost glow. "I'm gorgeous?" Had she looked like this before she got ill? She didn't think she had. No...she knew she hadn't. She'd been okay, maybe even pretty, but the creature who stared at her from the mirror was nothing short of stunning. "How...?"

"You were dying, Ambrosia." He stepped behind her, his reflection next to hers.

"And?"

"I—saved you."

"How? The doctors said there was no hope. I am—was going to die in a matter of days. And you say that's changed? That you *saved me?*"

"After finally finding you, I couldn't bear the thought of letting you die. I didn't want to lose you again." His image shrugged, the gesture echoed by the broad chest pressed against her back.

"How?" she hissed.

"I didn't get the chance to tell you everything about me before—can you please face me? I will show you everything."

"Show me?" She turned around, a welter of emotions fluttering inside her.

"Please, allow me." A shimmer of tears overtook the tender expression in his eyes. "I almost lost you." He cupped her cheeks with his palms and moved in, giving a gentle, slow-building kiss that sent a jolt of longing through her. Like a reflex, she welcomed him, her lips slowly parted, and their tongues curled and intertwined.

The same metallic flavor was in his mouth, too—then a flood of memories came rushing back. As if a curtain had lifted, she witnessed their blissful interludes just as they had happened, the many nights of dreamscaping to her lover, the tender kisses, and the taste, the memory of feeding from him shot a lightning bolt of desire through her chest.

"Desmond?" She reeled back. "I understand now. It *was* you, I remember. You saved me."

"Yes, but I didn't have the chance to explain first. I should have given you a choice."

She searched her memory further. "The metallic taste. Oh my God, the gypsy."

"Gypsy?"

"She talked about a copper-like taste, unconventional healing. She said we would meet, we would love, and I would live a different existence."

"Yes, it will be a very different existence, an eternal one." He reached for her and she coiled away from him.

"Eternal...copper...did you feed me blood?" Nausea made her swallow fast, to keep it down.... "I'm...what am I? What are you?

"I had no choice, please."

"You're a vampire?" Her eyes grew wide with horror.

"Yes."

"When you saved—you turned me?" She stumbled backward, bumping into the marble counter.

"Yes."

"I'm a vam—" She clasped her hands over her mouth.

"Ambrosia."

She backed away from him, slamming her hip into the door.

"Wait, don't go, please."

She spun and fled, out of the bathroom, the strangely beautiful underwater hotel room...and his life.

Chapter Five

*A*wash with grief, Desmond stared at the endless water for hours. He couldn't stand the thought of her hating him, for eternity, and he certainly couldn't follow through with his plan, no matter how much he wanted to give up and die. He had a responsibility to Ambrosia now, whether she ever spoke to him again or not. It would be cowardice to commit suicide, leaving her to fend for herself with her new immortality. She was already alone, but to start out with nothing, with no one at her side when she had to face the world as a vampire, he couldn't even consider this.

"Desmond, open the door." *Aldon.* Desmond dragged himself across the room and let him in.

"I knew I was wrong. I didn't have the right—"

"Everything is going to be okay now." Aldon smiled.

"How could you say that? She hates me." He walked back toward the ocean, wishing he could lose himself in its eternal depths.

"I wouldn't exactly say that."

He spun around in shock.

"Ambrosia?" Her figure cloaked by an overcoat, only her silky hair and stunning face were in view, but they were more than enough.

"Aldon explained everything."

A flurry of mixed emotions swallowed him up; ecstasy at seeing her again, terror of what she might think, and gratitude Aldon had had the sense to seek her out.

"You two need some time to—talk. I hear there's a fine lounge in this hotel. If you love birds will excuse me, there is a bottle of twenty-five year old bourbon calling to me. Yes, Ambrosia...you can still drink the occasional cocktail."

Before Desmond could respond, the fading vision of Aldon's back disappeared down the hall, followed by the sharp ding of the elevator and the sliding of the heavy metal doors closing. "Ambrosia, I'm so sorry—" He couldn't meet her eyes.

"Shhh." She came near and placed her finger on his lips to silence him. "It was a difficult thing for you to do. I realize that now."

"You should have had a choice—I didn't have the right—"

"Do you remember the last thing I said to you before I—before you had to save me?"

"Yes, I do." Desmond stood with his hands in his pockets and watched her brilliant green eyes with awe.

"I said I wished I had more time, so when you think about it, I inadvertently asked you to turn me. There was no other way for you to grant my desire."

"Well...I never explained...."

"You never told me, but you never denied being a vampire either."

"You never asked." He grimaced. Not that anyone ever would.

"Then we're even." She put her arms around his neck.

A flutter in his stomach was followed by a growing sense of relief and he slid his hands around her waist. "So, how did Aldon find you?"

"I suppose tracking down newborn vampires is a chore he has become accustomed to." Ambrosia gave a sheepish grin as she stared up at him sliding her fingers along the corners of her mouth as though she were wiping it clean.

"He found you in the hotel kitchen, didn't he?"

"Well, the meat locker, but I couldn't find anything appealing there, except the smell of blood."

"Right, no livestock." He chuckled. "You must be famished."

"Actually, we raided the medical clinic in town while we talked."

"Very resourceful." Desmond smiled.

"It was Aldon's idea. He knew I wouldn't be able to function if I didn't get some nourishment."

"I see." Desmond brushed her luxurious strawberry strands back from her face and caressed her cheek.

"And can you please explain to me, what was that thing he did—when he figured out where I was?"

"Oh, you mean the telepathy?"

"Yeah, that." She glowered.

"Annoying, isn't it?"

"I would agree with that. I couldn't hide from him because I heard his voice no matter how hard I tried to block out the sound."

Ambrosia trailed her fingers down his cheek, his throat and along his chest. "So, Desmond, I need you to answer just one more question for me tonight."

"What's that?"

"Since this is technically supposed to be a one-night stand, don't you think we should honor our arrangement?

"I believe that would be a big yes—and an unavoidable one at that." Desmond gripped her hips pulling her tight against his growing hard on. She cupped her hand over his bulge, sending a shockwave of desire through his loins.

Sliding her tongue along the razor-sharp tips of his fangs, she gasped at the stinging sensation as hers protruded for the first time, coupled with a surge of hunger for his touch. An acidic fluid leaked from her protruding teeth, sending a jolt of euphoria through her. Aldon had told her of the venom, but not of its effect upon her. A growing intensity took hold, enhanced by the lustful strokes of his steely fingers, the sensual brush of his powerful hands along the length of her body. Energy vibrating throughout her core heightened with each graze of his teeth along her flesh. Sensations and emotions she'd never experienced before took her prisoner and wouldn't let her go.

Ambrosia eased off the long overcoat, and grinned.

"Ambrosia, this garment—" He worshiped the satin material with exploring fingers.

"I saw it in the window of a gift shop and couldn't resist. You like?"

"Very much so, too bad it won't be on for long."

She swayed as he massaged her ass through the black negligee. The interludes on the astral plane had been wonderful, but the reality of being in his arms brought her amplified lust and passion beyond her wildest dreams "I have never been an aggressive person by nature."

"Every night we met, you were sweet and tender." Blazing a trail of seductive kisses along the length of her throat, his voice was gruff between bliss inducing suckles on her skin.

"So, there's something you should be aware of."

"What is it?" Pulling the strap down her shoulder, he devoured the nape of her neck.

"I think that part of me may have changed."

"What do you mean?" He remained focused on sampling every inch of her.

Ambrosia took hold of his hands, restraining them at his sides. Desmond stared down at her with wide eyes and raised brows.

"There's so much—energy flowing through me right now, I can't describe it. I want to bite you. I feel aggressive, but I don't want to hurt you. I'm excited and aroused, but afraid of my impulses. Does that make any sense at all?"

"Actually, it does."

"Really?"

"Yes it does. Since the moment you ran into me at the fair, I've experienced a magnetic pull. I want to claim you in every way possible. If I had allowed my animal instinct to take control, I could have physically hurt you, so I had to stay away, except on the astral level. Those meetings were incredible, but the physical pull when we're together is more—so much more."

"I've never experienced this sensation before. Is it a vampire thing?"

"I believe it's a soul mate thing. A part of each of us was missing, and when we found our other half, we naturally wanted to join in every way, almost consume one other."

"Yes, that's exactly it."

Letting out a dirty laugh, he pulled her hard against his solid, lean body.

She claimed the sweetness of his lips. Releasing his hands, she cradled his face, kissing him as he stroked her mouth to ecstasy with his talented tongue. Gripping lust consumed her. Desmond's ebony button-down shirt was a temporary deterrent until she flung it open, sending buttons flinging across the room, clinking as they bounced off the walls and the floor. Ambrosia explored the chiseled plains of his torso then moved her fingers down to the softness of the cotton material of his flat-front chino pants. Impatient, she ripped open the button and zipper. The feeble metal surrendered, parting like butter under her strength.

"Oh yeah." Desmond slid his pants down. "I think I could get used to this side of you."

He stood, naked, under her sexual reign, and she loved it. She trailed her fingers down the fine line of masculine hair trailing from his navel down to seventh heaven.

"Desmond?" She moved closer again.

"Yes?" His strong hands squeezed her breasts freeing them from the confines of their satin prison.

"Rip it off me."

Desmond tore the gown off, exposing her skin to the cool air of their underwater room.

"You turn me on so much." He grabbed her around the waist with one hand and clutched her breast with the other, pinching and twisting her pulsing nipple between his fingers.

"I want you, Desmond." Ambrosia grabbed his cock and massaged it to steely hardness.

"I aim to please." Desmond lifted her up with one arm around the small of her back and one supporting her ass. The stiffness of his dick rubbed along the inside of her thigh as she wrapped her legs around his waist.

Lost in the depths of his intoxicating kiss, she barely realized he'd carried her over to the desk until she felt the flatness of the wooden surface under her bare ass cheeks.

"I guess this is a night of firsts for both of us," Desmond's heavy breath at her ear sent chills down her spine.

How so?" She dragged her nails up the length of his defined back, smiling at his deep, blissful groan.

"I've never had such a hard time controlling myself before." Desmond tilted his head back and she followed his gaze to two sharks swimming overhead and a school of colorful fish rushing out of their way. "Do you think it's because we're under the sea?"

"Come to think of it...."Ambrosia felt behind her and swept everything off the desk then pulled him down with her. "It's a first for me too."

She trembled as he trailed kisses down her neck, along her abdomen, and suckled the inside of her thigh. A gasp of ecstasy slipped out when the sharpness of his fangs penetrated her flesh.

"Desmond—ah that feels amazing." She grabbed handfuls of his jet-black hair and guided him to her throbbing pussy. Ambrosia writhed at the sensation of his fingers parting her fleshy folds and his tongue flicking her clit repeatedly. Tantalizing swirls of her nub between his lips and teeth sent her reeling. He buried his finger deep inside her, stroking her to the brink of explosion, and just when the beginning of the spasms started, he pulled back leaving her gasping.

"What? Why did you stop?"

"When you come, I want you to explode in my mouth."

"Well, I can guarantee that's about to happen." She pulled his head back into place and wiggled her hips inviting his tongue to return. Sweeping the outside of her mound, he darted his tongue inside over and over again. Desmond rubbed his finger with exquisite tenderness over her clit in a circular motion. The vibrating spasm returned, stronger and more rapid now. Desmond sucked her clit and pounded his fingers into her. Her breathing sped up, her muscles tightened, and a white hot, molten sensation shot through her core as she contracted around his fingers in blissful spasms that rippled over her entire body.

"That's it, come for me, baby." He lapped up her juices eagerly. "Mmm, you taste so good." Ambrosia's body shook as she rode the waves of rapture.

"It's your turn now." She sat on the edge of the desk and pulled him to stand in front of her. Ambrosia stroked his cock, lowered her head, and then slid the rock hard tip into her mouth.

When Desmond moaned, she lifted her head and watched his expression when she cupped her breasts and pressed them together. "Fuck my tits."

Desmond gave a dark, sexy grin, and then gripped his rigid hard on and inserted it between her throbbing mounds. He slid his cock upward as she pressed her flesh tightly around his sinewy shaft.

"Desmond, wouldn't it feel good if it was slippery? Sliding between my breasts?"

"Yes."

"Grab that lotion out of the bathroom...." Before she could finish the sentence, he was back and dowsing her chest with the creamy white moisturizer. She gripped his cock again, rubbed it in the glob of cream then cupped her tits waiting for him to join her again. The fragrant aroma of lavender filled her nose.

Desmond moved forward with his hand gripping his steely tip and she swathed his shaft with her burgeoning flesh, squeezing tight as he moved his hips up and down in a rhythmic motion. With every thrust, she pressed tight, massaging his member with her aching breasts.

"That feels so good, ah—I don't wanna come yet." He slowed his pace down.

"You can come as many times as you want." She stood up, determined, facing him.

"I want to get inside you; I've wanted you for so long." He

cradled her face in his palms and devoured her lips with compelling lust. Their tongues danced and curled together endlessly while he lifted her up again, resting her against his hips. She wrapped her legs around him, eager to feel him enter her.

The cool, smoothness of the glass against her back surprised her when he pushed her up against the window. Ambrosia eased herself onto the tip of his cock, still kissing him, nipping at his lips and tongue.

She glimpsed the movement overhead, the sharks and schools of fish swimming all around them.

"Fuck me now." She nibbled on his earlobe.

In one vicious, sharp motion, he drove up into her, penetrating deep and hard. Ambrosia cried out with elation.

"Yes, I'm yours Desmond, fuck me," she begged him, gripping his shoulders. He thrust into her repeatedly; each drive harder than the last. A sharp squeaking sound began as her back rubbed up against glass. She buried her nails in his taut skin, arching her torso in a frenzy of yearning and tilting her hips toward him. She rode his cock relentlessly.

Desmond plunged into her rapidly, gripping her ass. The bounce of her breasts with every blissful movement of his pelvis shot waves of exhilaration over her.

His breathing grew harsh and ragged as he began gyrating his hips in a delicious, circular motion.

Her throbbing pussy clenched as a spasm exploded within her core, then rippled throughout her body. Her muscles contracted and she clung to his neck as she whimpered with delight.

"I can feel you coming Ambrosia. Ah, you're so tight. I'm gonna come."

"Yes, yes, come with me," she panted, riding waves of euphoria.

He clutched her ass hard as they collided in perfect primal rhythm. She pressed down to meet his every upward thrust while he pounded into her fiercely.

"Ah, here I come, ah, I'm—I'm—Ahhh, I'm coming." He

groaned loud and long, pulling her tight onto him with his final slamming thrusts of climax, he stiffened in release and exploded inside her. He shook violently as he held her on his pulsating cock. Shuddering, Desmond captured her trembling lips with his and squeezed her tight against his convulsing body.

"You're incredible."

"I would have to say the same about you." She clung to his neck as the residual spasm washed over her quivering body.

C3

Lying in bed, Desmond inhaled long and deep, cherishing her delectable scent and the feeling of her lying in his arms. Watching the aquatic life swim all around them was mesmerizing. Ambrosia's fingers tickled his chest and he took her hand into his, intertwining their fingers as they lay together, with only a sheet draped over them.

"If you had told me yesterday I'd be lying in bed with you, watching under the sea, I would have laughed." He grinned in satisfaction at the entire situation.

"If you had told me yesterday, I would be alive and pain free—"

"I'm so thankful Ambrosia. I really did think I lost you."

"I can't believe I couldn't remember you for all those months."

"Hey, look, there are our friends again." Desmond pointed to the pair of sharks swimming over the tunnel, waving their tails in unison.

"You know, before tonight, I thought sharks were scary."

"You did?" He ran his fingers through her golden mane while she rested her head on his chest.

"Yeah, I've always thought, they were cold-blooded killers."

"And now?"

"And now, I'm just like them." Her voice trailed off.

"Ambrosia, are you regretting this?"

"No, there's just so much I don't know, what to expect, how to—I've only ever heard about vampires in horror stories before.

It never dawned on me they were real."

"Well, if it helps, the horror stories are fables and superstition. There's a lot about us—me, that's pretty compassionate."

"The compassion, I have definitely experienced."

"There are some things that are different."

"Like what?" She sat up and watched him with her vibrant, emerald eyes.

"Like, when we mate, it's for eternity. We search until we find the one, and then no other will ever do."

"So the stories about sexually deviant vampires...?" She grinned up at him.

"Well, as you experienced tonight, sexual deviance is in our nature, just not promiscuity. We get down and dirty, but it's real."

"Does that go for all vampires?"

"I don't know, I haven't met them all yet." He laughed.

"You're teasing me aren't you?" She slapped his chest.

Desmond flipped her onto her back and pinned her to the bed with her hands over her head, giving her his most intense bedroom eyes. She quivered under his hands.

"Okay, so I'm feeling devious again."

Desmond watched her intently.

"What?" She furrowed her brows with a grin.

"Do you remember what you said to me earlier tonight?"

"What? I said a lot of things; you'll have to narrow it down for me a little." She giggled.

"You said, and I quote; *you can come as many times as you want, Desmond.*"

"I did? I don't remember." She frowned, but her eyes sparkled.

"Let me refresh your memory." Desmond descended on her lips, claiming their sweetness with ravenous hunger.

SAVANNAH'S GHOST TALE

BY

KALI WILLOWS

Chapter One

*O*rgasmic groans filled the air. "Oh my God, right there, wait—no—I don't it like there."

"Be patient. It has to hurt before it gets better. I promise, I'll be gentler. Just let me finish. I'm getting close. I can feel it."

"No, hold on, that hurts my—oh yeah, now you've got it."

"Good Lord, Vannah, will you keep it down over there? I'm trying to enjoy myself, too." Her sister's annoyed tone cut through the soft background music.

"Sorry, Stacia, no one has done this to me such in a long time. I'll try to shut up. It just feels so—oh—ah...." Vannah buried her face into the padded circle headrest.

"When was the last time you had a deep muscle massage, Ms. Teale?" The petite brunette masscuse tucked the sheet over Vannah's shoulder and moved to the other side.

"It's been so long I don't remember, Nadia, but you're doing great. Don't stop, please?"

"So, when is the big date?" Stacia's sly voice contracted Vannah's muscles again.

"Dammit, Stacia."

Taunting laughter from across the room resonated through her as she cringed under the painful kneading of her shoulder. While the visit to the hotel's luxurious spa had come with their stay, Vannah began to wish she'd just soaked in the huge bathtub in her room.

"Okay Nadia, I think that's as good as it's gonna get for me. Thank you." At her sharp tone, the woman packed up in a rush with shaky hands and excused herself.

Stacia sighed. "Justine, thank you so much. We have to get ready for the Ghost Walk tour soon." Sitting up, she secured her towel and hopped off the massage table, collecting her bag and retrieving a few bills from her wallet. "Please share this with Nadia; we both appreciate the great pampering."

"As you wish, Mrs. Leonard." The older, more seasoned masseuse accepted the cash and left the room.

"Well that was rude." Stacia spun around after the door closed, shooting a fiery glare at Vannah.

"I'm sorry, but for the love of God, do you have to broadcast that I'm getting laid? Shit." She stormed behind the mahogany paneled privacy screen. The flaring heat of her cheeks was unbearable. With a tense jaw, she scrambled into her clothing.

"My word, Vannah, you are way too sensitive about this. No one knows why you're here. People stay at hotels for all kinds of reasons. Your behavior, however, may send a clue or two about your agenda."

"What behavior?" She tugged her lace camisole over her head, wincing at the sound of a thread popping in the delicate pink garment.

"You know what I mean. You're snapping and barking at anyone who tries to show you some good old Southern hospitality."

"I'm not snapping at anyone." Jamming her pedicured foot into her sandal, she cringed as the heel strap began to tear.

"Oh yeah? What about the bellhop?"

"He grabbed my hand."

"He was collecting your suitcase." A low, admonishing tone took over Stacia's words.

"Well he didn't have to rip it from me."

"Uh huh."

"Okay, and the desk clerk? I smiled at him when we checked

in."

"You clenched your teeth and reprimanded him for calling you madam."

"Well—" Flustered, she searched her brain for an excuse for her out-of-character rudeness. "They shouldn't be allowed to call anyone under eighty years old *madam*."

"Okay, you're either getting hungry or need to get plastered." Stacia surveyed herself in the mirror, wearing her new, blue summer dress and sandals, running her brush through her long, blonde locks—perfectly lovely as always.

Vannah dropped into the posh ivory sling back chair behind her.

Stacia's penetrating gaze softened as she pulled a stool close. Vannah caught the reflection of her blotchy red eyes and swollen upper lip in the bronzed mirror on the wall. Her sister was a carbon copy of herself, the same flaxen curls trailing down her chest, and the gold flecks within the chestnut brown of her almond shaped eyes. They could easily pass for twins, although Vannah was two years younger. But Stacia always seemed happy, her full lips curled up into a sensational smile, her face alight with a youthful glow. Vannah saw a dark, strained, lesser version of her stunning sister in her own reflection.

"Honey, it's been three years—it's not unfaithfulness, it's moving on with your life in the easiest way possible." Stacia's calm tones did not soothe her this time.

"Easiest?"

"You, my darling, are a strong, vivacious, beautiful, passionate—"

The sides of Vannah's mouth began to retreat from their purse and her brows raised a little.

"—bitter, angry, desolate woman." Stacia finished.

The words sliced like daggers through her broken heart. "Thanks a lot."

"I've watched you lock yourself into an emotional prison cell ever since you lost Mark, but enough is enough."

"That's easy for you to say. You have a husband who loves

you—you have everything you need." Her head rolled back as she exhaled through gritted teeth. Shocked at her own insensitivity, she looked back at Stacia and softened her tone. "Almost everything. I'm sorry. I can be a real ass sometimes."

"Those are just the cards I was dealt and you, of all people, should know that can change in a heartbeat. You had a good thing with Mark, honey. You'll find that again sooner than you think."

"Well, maybe I don't want it. Did that ever occur to you?" Vannah jumped up and stomped across the room. The blue depths of the Savannah River out of the open window did nothing to soothe her internal torment.

"No, it hasn't. And I'll tell you why, little sister."

Tears streamed down Vannah's heated cheeks.

"When you were with Mark, you were the happiest person I knew. You were—you. Since the night he died, I don't even recognize you anymore. You want to be happy again. I know you do. You're just scared to death that you will be."

"You seem to know so much. Why am I scared of being happy?" Nasal words spewed from her mouth as the wetness streamed down her face and neck.

"Because you're terrified of getting hurt all over again."

She was startled by the tender grasp on her shoulders, Vannah tried to hold back the heart-wrenching sobs that surged out of her tight throat and trembling lips. Stacia always knew how to access her buried emotions. *Dammit.*

With loving arms wrapped around her from behind, Vannah gripped Stacia's folded fingers, and held tight as she broke down, Stacia's strength—true to form—was her salvation.

"You're gonna get through this, Vannah. I promise. One day soon. For now, you're gonna start with your date. Madame Evangeline is renowned for her matchmaking abilities."

"Fine." She sniffed and pulled away, avoiding her sister's burrowing stare.

"Besides, staying at the Castillo Plantation is quite the honor—a brand new hotel in Southern Savannah? Come on, how can we not make the most of it?"

"We should grab a bite to eat before the ghost walk." Vannah ran her trembling fingers across her wet face as she gathered her belongings from the chair.

"I guess you're right."

Vannah opened her camel brown leather Gucci tote and sorted through her electronic arsenal.

"Oh Jesus, you're not doing that tonight are you?"

"Yes."

"What if there are families on the walk?

"What if there are?"

"You'll scare the crap out of them. This is supposed to be fun and light entertainment."

"I can be fun."

"Sure you can, on America's Most Wanted Ghouls and Goblins."

"Oh, you're hilarious."

"You're gonna embarrass me again, aren't you?"

"Would I do that?"

Stacia followed her across the room, mocking her with a sarcastic pucker as Vannah held the door open.

"Dinner?" Vannah gave her disgruntled sister a triumphant smirk.

"Sure and maybe I'll buy you a drink—or five. Do you think that might take the edge off your ghost hunting?" Soft chuckles sounded down the elaborate wood paneled hallway as they sauntered to the elevator.

ଓ

"Uh—thank you for dinner, Cameron. It was—interesting." His latest attempt at a date hurried to her charcoal LeSabre and hopped in.

"Janet, I'm sorry about the—interruption. Can I make it up to you another time?"

"The thing is, Cameron, you're an attractive guy. Funny. Charming. But I can't see you again." She turned the key in the

201

ignition, avoiding his probing stare.

"But Janet."

"Don't call me; this is just too weird." She clicked her seat belt.

"Your mom said she won't butt in again," he offered with desperation.

Janet's jaw dropped. He could have sworn she turned a little white, too, before the purr of the engine became a roar and the sound of squealing tires left him standing by the curb with burning rubber stinging his nose.

"Well, that went better than the last one. At least she didn't throw anything at me." With heavy shoulders, he stood on the edge of the cobblestone sidewalk, staring at the still smoking black skid marks on the pavement.

The muffled hum in his ear was of no consolation. "Sorry Cameron, maybe I should have warned you that she's scared of ghosts and the whole life after death idea?" Doris's soft voice filled his head with gentle laughter. Her apology offered no solace.

"Yeah, yeah, shoulda, coulda, woulda. I know, *you didn't mean to.* How many times have I heard that before from every spirit that drops in for just a minute? I might as well pledge my celibacy to the church and become a monk as long as you dead guys—and ladies—keep hanging around." Doris's presence evaporated when the muffled sound of Vincent Price's laughter sang out from his pocket.

Letting out a heavy sigh, he hit the talk button. "Hello? Hey Samuel.... How did it go? Oh, well, this one was much better. No bruises and no police were called."

Chapter Two

"That was pretty amazing. I've never had fried green tomatoes before." Stacia heaved a sigh and settled back into her seat. "Come to think of it, I've never eaten maggot-infested, eel either." She frowned when she got no response. "Vannah!"

"What?"

"Put that away."

Vannah continued to fumble through her bag. "I have to get it ready; the tour is in an hour."

"You have some serious issues. Who goes for an entertaining ghost walk with an EMF detector and an infrared camcorder? Seriously?" Stacia flung her napkin on the table and shot a glare of questioning disapproval.

"A ghost hunter. Hello?"

"Self-proclaimed ghost hunter."

"Hey, I'm a professional now."

"You're a professional pain in the ass, sweetheart." Stacia rolled her head back and huffed with frustration.

"Do you not remember the episode of *Ghost Hunters* I was on last year?"

"You mean the one where you stood on the side watching the cast take readings and trace objects on paper?"

"Hey, I don't appreciate your cynicism, thank you very much."

"Vannah, your obsession with the dead has gotten out of

control."

"My obsession is with proving there is no such thing." Vannah fussed with her detector checking the battery.

"Whatever. Just don't make people uncomfortable tonight. Most people go for entertainment. Don't spoil it for others like you did last time."

"That couple never should have been in there to begin with." Vannah's shoulders edged up toward her ears as her inflection rose.

"Part of the tour of the gallows was to take pictures in the cell, Vannah, not get locked in with the lights out while some freak beams infrared cameras at you."

"I apologized. Besides, she didn't need stitches."

"Ugh!"

"All right, I'll be more discreet this time."

Stacia settled back into her chair and grinned at her. "So, when is the big date anyway?"

"The date, oh—not until tomorrow night. Nine o'clock." She grimaced.

"Maybe once you get a little somethin' you'll stop obsessing so much."

Vannah glowered at her.

"I'm just saying."

"Stacia, my wallet's not in here." Vannah rummaged through her bag, frenzied.

"Did you leave it at the spa?"

"I don't think so."

"We can check there in the morning, I'll cover dinner." Stacia pulled out her credit card and placed it on the little plastic tray with the bill. "Maybe, just to be on the safe side, we should report your cards missing."

"I'll go to the front desk and have them contact the credit card company. Thanks." Vannah's brows pressed tight together as she tried to figure out the mystery.

"What is it Vannah?"

"It's just that I'm sure I had it when we started dinner." She bent over, pulling the cloth up and searched under the table.

ℭ𝔰

"Thank you for joining our tour. My name is Cameron Evans."

Vannah kept her tote on her shoulder, pulled close like a security blanket.

"Now, this tour is narrated by your guide—uh—that would be me—" He flashed a toothy grin, "—I'm an historian-intuitive, folklorist, master storyteller, and native Georgian who has grown up learning the legends—" eyeing the group members, he offered a sinister voice with a chuckle, "—that lie beneath the haunting tales of Savannah."

"Yeah, right." Vannah hiked her bag higher on her tight shoulder.

"Shhh." Stacia gave her a push.

"We'll explore the in-depth, informative, and spookier shades of this lovely city's haunted history. We believe this is a spine-tingling tour that even the skeptic will enjoy." His infiltrating gaze caught her attention coupled with his devilishly charming smile.

"Our haunted Ghost Walk is filled with stories from Savannah's spectral past. You'll hear tales of poltergeists, shadow people, voodoo, and more!"

"So is all of this malarkey based on actual research, or do you come up with this crap on your own?" The venomous words prompted several heads to turn toward the back of the crowd.

"Vannah." Stacia jabbed a sharp elbow to her right side.

"Sorry," She rubbed her ribs.

"Folks...." His deep voice drew their attention back to the front.

"I mean it, I'm gonna clock you," Stacia shot a stern glare at her. *"Behave."*

"Fine."

"Savannah is often described as charming, captivating, and even sultry, but it's also well known for its dark, mysterious side."

Vannah leaned forward, inspecting the know-it-all's broad shoulders and striking, chiseled features.

"Wow, he's hot," Stacia purred.

"If you're into that sort of thing." Vannah's gaze dropped to her French-manicured nails.

"Sure, who's into thick, luscious, deep blond hair that you could tangle your fingers in? Or, the six foot four, athletic Greek Adonis type who looks like he could rock your boat all night long?"

"Stacia!"

"What? Did you get a glimpse of that ass in those shorts, his legs, and solid muscles? And there isn't much left to the imagination under that skin tight tank top. Those impeccable arms, his rock-hard pecs, his bulging—"

"Stop it."

"But that beautiful, bronzed tan—"

"Enough, you want to get a room with him or something?"

"Touchy touchy, me doth think thou protest too much, dear sister." Stacia poked a tickling finger into her waist.

"Would you grow up already?"

"Ladies, are you still joining us?" A velvet voice hummed over Vannah's shoulder, sending chills down her spine.

The bantering duo paused, and Vannah turned around, realizing everyone else had already begun walking ahead.

"Yes, we're still coming—I mean walking." Vannah stuttered as flaring heat ran over her cheeks.

"That's good; I wouldn't want you to miss it." With a seductive wink, he waved at the street before them.

"After you, ladies."

They walked alongside him until they caught up to the rest. A slow, sultry breeze blew a sweeping whiff of woody musk cologne past her nose. For the first time on this trip, Vannah was speechless.

Stopping beside her, he continued his spiel. "Savannah is recognized by many as America's most haunted city."

Although she would never admit it out loud, Vannah found the long, winding cobblestone streets filled with a fascinating sense of the past. The simple elegance of an earlier era, augmented by the lingering smell of wet pavement from the drizzling rain earlier that evening, made her feel as if she'd stepped back in time.

Antebellum homes showcased picket fences, massive trees, and lavish, colorful gardens. They sauntered past historic plantation estates while savoring the sultry night air. Strolling through the squares of the picturesque town, she admired the Spanish moss-draped, majestic oaks that lined the streets. Everything seemed so whimsical, in a dark and dreary kind of way.

When the divine aroma of roses cascaded around her, Vannah inspected the foliage she was passing, and saw no blossoms of any kind. The mossy oaks at her side were accompanied only by green shrubs. She turned around at a tap on her shoulder, but saw no one behind her. Stacia was within arm's reach, however.

"Stop it. That's not funny."

"What?" Stacia stared ahead, focused on their guide.

Vannah took a few more steps and a muffled sound vibrated in her ear. Catching her breath, she shot a glare at Stacia. "I mean it. Knock it off."

"What?"

"Yeah, right. Don't do it again."

"Do what?" Stacia hissed with annoyance.

"Oh, never mind."

Slight shivers rolled over Vannah's heated skin and a soft rush of bliss rippled through her inner core for a brief moment. Her pelvic muscles squeezed and released as though she had an involuntary Kegel movement. Vannah shuddered from the sensation then continued without giving it another thought.

In the shadowy nighttime, the adventure of following Cameron and the posse down the old, haunted footpaths, listening to the city's legends, drew her attention away from the gadgets in her bag. She'd become distracted from her agenda of disproving the spectral hysteria.

"...into the 'tween places that mark the stealthy passageways from the known, into the unknown."

The guide's captivating voice and storytelling brought about a curiosity she hadn't prepared for. His tales were believable; she could feel the history, the suggested looming presence of times past, and her openness to it was unacceptable. No, she wouldn't lose sight of her reason for being there. Vannah eased her fingers through the interior of her bag, noting that Stacia was preoccupied staring at Adonis who stood at an entrance way of a graveyard, hypnotizing his groupies.

The tour had stopped for another haunting legend...yada yada yada.

"This centuries-old cemetery is believed to be frequented by the spirits who, the Geechee-Gullah say, stand at their graves in a midnight ritual. The Yamacraw Indian, Irish, and Geechee-Gullah folk believe the unseen can tap us on our shoulders and whisper in our ears."

Sure they can. Vannah backed away with her camcorder in hand and snuck through the side gate of the graveyard. Staying close enough that she could still hear him ramble on about dusky tunnels and eerie tombstones, Vannah turned on her infrared camera and began scanning the ancient gravestones. A distant mausoleum caught her attention. Although nothing showed on the device, she was certain she caught the movement of something in front of that building.

Cautious of being seen, she held her camera ready and inched along the fence toward the faded monument. The small, stone, Parthenon-style structure was swathed with shaggy, green moss and woody vines. Vannah's heart skipped a beat when she observed the door was ajar.

"Hey Cameron?" A whisper in his ear distracted him from his cemetery tale.

"Okay, who are you? I'm kinda in the middle of something here." Cameron mentally scolded his uninvited ghostly guest as the tourists began to disperse, snapping photos of the statues along the front of the antiquated burial grounds.

"It would appear you have a stray." The voice was male, but not identifying himself for the moment.

The picturesque blonde caught his eye as she ducked behind the stone wall off the side gate to the graveyard.

"What do you suppose she's up to in there?"

"Go find her before she gets into trouble." The voice faded as Cameron's brother approached.

"Avid ghost hunter?" Samuel sighed.

"Maybe, but she's gonna keep me busy tonight, I suspect. Tag team?"

"Sure, I got this story covered." Samuel moved to the head of the tour group as Cameron slipped away to track down his renegade spectator.

A beautiful woman in a dark graveyard; this could end badly. A few flashes of what was to come filled his head, a little goad from his haunted helper.

With slow, deliberate steps, Vannah climbed the soil-laden stairs to the doorway, ready to peer inside. The musty odor of plant decay filled the air. A vibration erupted in her hand and her heart pummeled against the confines of her chest. The camera screen went blank.

"Dead battery? But I just charged it. Dammit."

The stagnant, humid air grew frosty. Goose bumps surfaced all over her bare legs and arms. Even her nipples hardened to scrape against her sheer camisole with the chilly air. She gripped her camera and scanned around her, amazed to see her exhaled breath materialize into a cloudy, gaseous state.

A cold front? She struggled to convince herself.

The overpowering fragrance of roses caressed her nose again. A quick glance showed still no flowers nearby, and then a soft brushing against her hardened nipples startled her. Wintry pressure gripped her erect peaks. Her eyes closed and her head swayed back as a delectable force began to condense around her breasts. Mesmerized by the exquisite sensation, her arms went limp with the camera still in her grip, allowing the cold to consume her flesh.

A gentle icy grazing ran across her lips, down the length of her throat, and along the lace of her blouse. Chilling tingles surfaced over her scalp and spread down the back of her neck, rolling over her entire body. A buzzing sensation began on her inner thighs and climbed upward. Her legs began to part as frosty pinching aroused her and her pelvic muscles contracted. Her body pushed down, welcoming the sensation, and a low building groan erupted from her throat.

The sound of her own voice awakened her from the trance, and the pounding of her heart returned her to acute awareness. Vannah shoved the camera in her purse and pulled out the EMF detector. Her teeth chattered as she turned it on, holding it in front of her like a loaded gun. The ghost hunter's fear soared as the needle darted back and forth for a few seconds then stopped dead.

What the hell is going on? A shadow flashed across the stone threshold, startling her. Her heart raced and she stumbled down the steps, her eyes flitting frantically back and forth, scanning for movement but finding none. Her clumsy feet tangling, she stumbled over a flat stone and toppled backward.

A sudden heat surrounded her and she paused in mid-fall, suspended over the dark pit of an open grave. Breathless and terror-stricken, it took her a moment to realize the warmth was strong arms wrapped around her. Back on her feet, she spun around to find Cameron, the tour guide, watching her with an amused expression.

"Are you okay?" He gripped her shaking shoulders.

"I'm fine, I just saw—I tripped." Vannah tried to catch her breath, her mind racing with madness.

"You should watch where you're stepping in a cemetery."

"I didn't expect—I didn't realize they still buried people here."

"You know, it's frowned upon to be raiding graves at night around these parts."

"I wasn't raiding anything." She jerked out of his hold and grabbed her bag from the ground, jamming her detector back inside. *I'm glad none of my equipment ended up in that grave.* She yanked her twisted camisole top and shorts back into place.

"What did you see?" His penetrating gaze sent a current through her chest.

"Nothing, I didn't—there's nothing to see, let's go."

"Whoa, whoa, hang on. Something scared you. Tell me what

you saw."

If she wasn't throbbing with terror right now, she might have actually swooned under his gaze. "Are you deaf? I said I didn't see anything." She turned to walk away.

"Who is Mark?"

With a white hot jolt, her stomach bottomed out and her feet froze to the ground.

"Who is Mark and why can't he breathe? His chest burns." Cameron stepped in front of her, blocking her retreat and rubbing his torso with a contorted expression.

"Where did you—Stacia. I'm gonna kill her." She gulped a mouthful of stagnant, humid air.

"He's here, you know. That's what you saw." He spoke with a tender voice.

"This is a horrible joke. Just stop it." She pushed past him then stormed off to the group.

"Are you okay? What the hell were you doing?" Her sister's tone held concern, but she wasn't up to explaining.

"I'll deal with you later."

"What did I do?" Stacia grabbed her arm.

"I said, later."

"What the hell were you doing in the graveyard anyway?"

"Drop it." She yanked out of Stacia's grip and spun away, too upset to do anything else.

Cameron walked up to Vannah and paused with what seemed an apologetic expression before continuing over to the chatting spectators and resumed his narration to the group.

"Many people bought estates here, a while back, thinking they would be the ideal summer homes, but most packed up and left after hearing the laughter of children in empty hallways, feeling invisible fingers caress their faces, and seeing pale girls who seem to float through their gardens. This street became known for its abandoned houses until the city stepped in and preserved them."

He carried on with this farce of a Ghost Walk without so much as glancing her way again. He talked about folklore and legends like he believed in his own stories of the dead.

"Why is old Savannah's atmosphere so charged with paranormal energy? Why does it seem to draw its spirits back home?" The enthralled onlookers were a bunch of mindless idiots listening to the rants of an egomaniac.

The eerie aura of the darkened streets was creeping her out. His stories were just making it worse. What had she seen? What happened to her body in there? Residual throbs reverberated deep in her core.

"One famous citizen was revered for his lavish parties...."

Are you kidding me? This; *lonely souls wandering eternally, searching for unrequited love,* bogus was getting thin, and so was her patience.

"According to folklore, Room 204 in that hotel over there is haunted. A man's ghost is often sighted walking the halls and standing at the end of the bed, even running bath water and flushing toilets."

She'd promised Stacia not to draw any more attention to herself tonight—the lingering shivers of fright were a reminder to obey, but she wanted to give him a piece of her mind.

"...creeping in eerie courtyards, waiting for help to cross over...."

"Vannah?"

"I don't want to hear it, Stacia."

"No, Vannah, I—"

"Seriously, shut *up.*"

"I don't feel good."

Stacia's face was flushed. Beads of perspiration covered her forehead and ran down her temples, and the plunging neckline of her summer dress was dark with saturation as if sweltering heat consumed her.

Vannah's anger evaporated as her sister reached for her arm.

"Oh, I'm gonna be sick." Stacia cupped her mouth, staggered to the side of the walkway, and retched over the picket fence edging the sidewalk.

"Oh, God, was it the food?" Vannah hovered, holding Stacia's hair back as she heaved.

Stacia's convulsing slowed and then stopped. She stepped back and crouched, gasping for air.

"Everything's getting hazy." Vannah struggled to steady her, but Cameron scooped her up into his arms, as her body went limp.

"Sorry, folks, a lady in distress. My associate will continue the tour. Samuel, can you please see to our guests?" Without waiting for an answer from the good-looking, fair haired man at the foot of the crowd, he began walking back the way they'd come.

Vannah scrambled after him.

"What are you doing?"

"She needs to lie down. She needs some cool water."

"Wait, where are you going?"

"My place is around the corner."

"Shouldn't we take her to the hospital?" Vannah choked out the words through her tightened throat. She worked to hold back the tears collecting at the rims of her eyes as she step-hopped, trying to keep up with him.

"She's gonna be okay. Trust me."

"But what if it's food poisoning?" She tugged at his shirt.

Cameron looked at her with sapphire eyes aglow. "It's not food poisoning. Come on, we need to get her cooled down." He continued on, focused and unyielding.

ଔ

Vannah sat on the hard limestone floor, watching her sister toss and turn on Cameron's sofa. Fear raced in her heart, and her own skin was moist from the humid night air.

Cameron carried in a tray and placed it on the wicker table beside them. "Here's some water, a cold cloth, and a thermometer."

"Thermometer?"

"She's burning up, but she's gonna be fine." He kneeled beside Vannah and eased the device into Stacia's mouth.

Vannah watched with her lips pressed tight and panic rushing though her as he retrieved the beeping stick and examined it.

"A hundred and two; we have to get her cooled down." He held up the small towel. "Sponge her with this while I run a bath."

"Bath?"

As he passed her the damp cloth, warmth from his fingers against her palm jarred her heart and sent a rabble of butterflies dancing in her stomach.

ᛒ

An hour later, Stacia was sitting up on the white wicker couch, puffy red cushions under and tucked all around her. She held a glass of lemonade and Vannah's hand.

"You had me scared."

"I'm sorry, kiddo." She put the glass to her pale lips and sipped.

"So, how's our patient?" Cameron entered carrying a plate of crackers and cheese.

"Better, thank you, I'm sorry I ruined the tour."

"Nonsense, that was almost the last place. Besides, Samuel was there to finish up. Most of them were locals and have seen everything already anyway."

"Samuel?"

"Yeah, he's my older brother and business partner in the Haunted Ghost Walk. We take turns leading the tours and he does most of the business stuff. He calls me 'the talent.'" Cameron smirked a little.

"Thank you for helping my sister."

"It was my pleasure, madam." With smiling eyes, he gave a little nod and winked.

Vannah cringed—there was that word again.

"So, Stacia, how long have you known?" He placed his palm over her flat belly.

Stacia gasped. "How did you know?"

He smiled and pulled his hand away.

"Know what?" Vannah demanded.

"About a week. I haven't told anyone except my husband, not even—" She met Vannah's probing stare and shrugged.

"Know *what*?"

Stacia smiled as she rubbed her palms over her tummy.

"Honey, how do you feel about being called Aunt Vannah?"

"What? I thought you couldn't after the last...."

"I know. It's a miracle." Stacia was glowing. She stared at Cameron. "How did you know?"

"I—uh—heard it from uh—a friend." He glanced over his shoulder at the empty, arched doorway.

Stacia's voice lowered. "Who?"

"Well—I guess there's no avoiding it." He sighed, "Mark."

"What?" Vannah jumped up. "What the hell are you two doing?"

"I get that response from a lot of people," he lamented with a grimace.

"What do you mean?" Stacia's calm voice infuriated Vannah.

"I'm a psychic, or clairvoyant, medium, whatever you want to call it. I can see and hear the dead." Moving to the maroon armchair by the window, he sat on the edge of the seat facing Vannah. He kept his eyes fixed on hers.

"Psychic?" She crossed her arms over her chest.

"Yeah, I get that response a lot, too."

"Mark is here?" Stacia twisted her head to look in the darkened corners of the room.

"What the hell? Is this some perverse way to get me to move on? It's sick. Stop it, right now!" Vannah backed toward the door.

"Savannah Grace Teale." Cameron stood up and moved toward her.

"What did you call me?" She froze. The fragrance of roses returned, along with the shivers down her scalp and spine.

"I know you don't want to believe me, but I'm asking, no, I'm begging you, please just sit down and hear me out."

"Vannah, no one ever called you by your full name, except...." Stacia's voice trembled.

"Please. Just five minutes and I swear to God, I'll never bother you again."

Compelled by his pleading voice, Vannah walked over to the wicker couch and sat beside Stacia.

"Thank you." He took a seat on the brown leather ottoman

facing them.

His stare fixed on her, filled with empathy and remorse.

"Vannah, this gift—ability of mine, I've had my whole life, and I can't just turn it off at will. Mark has been communicating with us, non-stop, all night long."

"Us?" Her anger and confusion were matched now.

"He's been trying to get your attention, but, he says you're just as stubborn now as you always were."

"That sounds like Mark." Stacia's nervous laugh fell into silence.

"What are you talking about?" Her throat grew thick, making speech difficult.

"The smell of roses, the tap on your shoulder, the whisper in your ear. He said he even moved your wallet tonight to get your attention. When you got spooked at the cemetery, that incident at the mausoleum? That was Mark, the cold air, the moving shadow, the electrical problems with your gadgets—all him."

"I *lost* my wallet." She side-stepped the rest of his inarguable points. The suggestion that he knew what happened to her at the mausoleum shot searing heat through her cheeks and her pulsing veins.

"Check your bag—it's there now." He nodded to the tote by her feet.

"This is ridiculous."

"Vannah, check it." Stacia nodded with encouragement.

Vannah huffed and picked up her bag, rifling through it then paused when her heart jumped up to her throat. She pulled out the missing wallet.

"I'm not faking this. He needed to tell you something."

"What?" Half hopeful, she waited.

"He said, your date...tomorrow...he wants you to go through with it. Madame Evangeline knew what she was doing when she matched you. It's time to let him go. He wants you to start living again."

"Wow." She shook her head. Sitting back, she stared up at the domed ceiling.

"What, honey?" Stacia squeezed her wrist.

"Wow, you guys are good."

"What?"

"How long have you been planning this, Stacia? What did you do, hire an actor?" Vannah pulled her hand away, glaring at Cameron.

"I did no such thing." Stacia reached again for her but she resisted, avoiding any contact.

"Sure, like you didn't steal my wallet earlier and put it back just now? Like you didn't tap me on the shoulder earlier? You didn't put me up to this whole date business?"

"Vannah?"

"No, you crossed the line."

"There's something else." Cameron stood and walked toward her.

"Okay, Cameron, if that's even your real name, what else does *Mark* have to say?"

"He says you've been carrying a guilty secret since that night."

A shockwave of mixed fear, rage, and anguish rushed over her all at once, setting every atom of her body ablaze.

"Shut up. Not another word." She got up, clutching her bag to her chest.

"Okay, no more words, but I want you to do something for me." He stepped closer to her, peering at her face.

"Oh you do, huh? What's that?"

"I want you to take out your camera and other gadgets. I want you to record and take readings. When you go back to the Castillo Hotel, take time to review the data. Decide for yourself if this is real or not."

"Vannah?" Stacia called to her.

Vannah gaped at her calm sister in disbelief.

"Do it. For your own peace of mind—I dare you." Stacia knew how to push her buttons. A challenge to her skepticism was enough to boil her blood.

Vannah reached into her bag and whipped out her camera. She turned it on, expecting a dead battery, but the indicator noted a full charge. Pressing the record button, she scanned the room. Cameron nodded toward the open windows and Vannah aimed it there, too. A gust of arctic air rushed through her shaking body.

A tap on her shoulder sent her reeling around, but no one stood behind her. An inaudible muffle in her ear erupted again as she spun back, facing them, "Stacia, let's go." She spoke low and firm, trying to keep her voice even and hold back the cries of anguish that festered deep inside.

Stacia preceded her out of the room.

છ

"Um, that went well." Cameron heaved a sigh as the apparition brushed past him.

"I didn't think she would be so difficult to convince with everything you shared."

"Somehow Mark, I don't imagine this is a big surprise to you? She strikes me as an obstinate, opinionated woman who sticks to her guns."

"You've got that right. Spectacular, isn't she?" Cameron could feel Mark's lingering passion for her.

"To tell the truth, she's a pain in the ass. Stubborn, unreasonable—" He paused.

"And?" The playful specter egged him on.

"Magnificent."

The vivid image of her deep brown almond shaped eyes pierced through his vision.

"All right Mark, knock it off. I get the point."

Cameron stood in the empty doorway, the spirit gone again.

"As if she were going to come back after that."

છ

"So, how long before you talk to me?" Stacia called through the hotel room door. "Please don't leave a pregnant woman in distress. Open up."

Vannah turned the lock and pulled the door open, staring at the floor.

"Did you sleep at all? You look like shit." Stacia meandered into the room.

"Thanks a lot." She dawdled over to the bed and plopped her disheveled self down.

"So, what's the verdict, ghost hunter? Is he a fraud?" Stacia stood in front of her with a taunt in her tone.

"Stacia?"

"Yeah?"

"I'm only gonna ask you once, and I want the truth, no matter what."

Kneeling in front of her, she took Vannah's hands into hers. "What is it honey? You know I've never lied to you, I won't start now, I promise."

"Did you set this up? Cameron, I mean—did you tell him those things? Did you take my wallet and put it back?"

"Of course not. I would never hurt you like that. Did you review the images from last night?"

Vannah hung her head and exhaled. "Yes, I did."

"And?"

"Readings like I've never seen since I got the stupid thing."

"Then it was really Mark?"

"Maybe—I don't know—unless you're playing me, there's no other explanation."

"I'm not. Will you go back and talk to Cameron?"

"I don't think so."

"Why? You still don't believe him?"

"I think I do. But after my behavior last night, I'm too embarrassed. I was awful to him."

"I'm sure he understands how difficult this was for you."

"Maybe before we leave. I don't know."

"Will you still go through with your date tonight? I'm sure Madame Evangeline would understand if you backed out, given the circumstances."

"No. It's time. Even if I don't enjoy myself, it's a first step, one

I've avoided for too long."

"That's my girl." Stacia stood up pulling Vannah with her, and hugged her tight.

"Well, maybe I should try and nap or something. I'm exhausted." Vannah's deflated anger came as a relief.

"Where are you meeting? Never mind. Have fun and call my room if you need me."

Stacia headed for the door.

"Where are you going?"

"I'm kinda craving those fried green tomatoes they serve around here, and maybe some pickles, ice cream.... Who knows? I'm starving." Stacia's complexion glowed.

"How long has Charlie known about the baby?"

Stacia stopped holding the door handle with the most blissful look Vannah had ever seen on her face. "We took the test together right before I left to meet you."

"I'm happy for you both Stacia, it's been a difficult time for you."

"It's been a long wait for happiness for you, too, kiddo. Just remember something for me, okay?"

"What's that?"

"Life is too short to waste on regrets. You're being given a golden opportunity here to move on with your life. Use it well."

"I'll do my best, Stacia. Thank you."

"I love ya, kiddo."

"I love you too, but you're still a pain in my ass." One side of Vannah's mouth retreated as she shot her a half reprimanding look.

☙

Vannah paused in front of the oak-trimmed penthouse door and slowed her breathing. Her nerves were wreaking havoc on her stomach and her chest. Holding her breath, she knocked on the door of Room 1213.

The clicking sound of the turning lock caused a stir in her stomach. The door creaked open, and a woody scent of musk enveloped her senses. Vannah clutched the frame to stay upright when she saw who opened it.

"What the hell are you doing here?"

"Won't you come in, madam?"

"Stop calling me madam." She brushed past him.

Locking the door, he turned with a sheepish grin.

"Did you know it was me?" She dropped her bag on the royal blue and white Scalamandre silk chaise and sat down beside it.

"Not exactly—well, aside from the ghost telling me, it wasn't hard to guess. I doubt there's too many dates set up here in Savannah tonight by Eve."

"I don't think I can do this—not with you." She shook her head and clasped her clammy hand over her face.

The hot little red dress with the spaghetti straps and low cleavage was a most definite regret now. So was the sexy, black, lacy lingerie underneath.

"Yeah, I get that response a lot, too." He chuckled and settled on the cobalt chair across from her.

"You do?" She shot him a questioning glance.

"Yeah, it's amazing how ghosts can mess with your love life or make it non-existent. Most often I can't get through the first course in a restaurant without some spirit jumping in for a message or two."

"So—this isn't the first time this has happened to you?" Careful with her revealing hemline, Vannah crossed her feet at the ankles and kept her legs pressed together, folding her fingers and draping them over her clenched knees.

"Nope, that's why I agreed to 1Night Stand."

"What do you mean you agreed?"

"Well, big brother Samuel thought I needed a break from the failed dating scene."

An awkward silence filled the room.

"What did you find on the video footage?" A one-sided smirk lit up his confident stare.

"What do you think I found?" Vannah leaned forward, challenging him. "You said I was carrying a guilty secret?"

"Uh—yeah, about that...." he stammered.

"What?"

"I guess there's nothing to lose tonight anyway, so I'll spill."

"I'm waiting." She tapped her stiletto heel.

"Are you sure you want to do this now?" Concern filled his voice.

"Yes." She wasn't sure, but a brave appearance was called for.

The familiar fragrance of roses blew in with a gentle breeze. Vannah glanced at the closed window and shuddered. The compelling flower scent lingered about her.

"Please, Cameron. Tell me."

"Okay, here it goes. Mark says you've been ghost hunting to bury your grief. You felt if—"

"If what?" The stinging tears began to form, but she held her posture upright.

"If you couldn't find proof that ghosts existed, then he couldn't be angry with you—he wouldn't blame you for the fire."

"Why would I think he blamed me?"

"He says you; you had wine, dinner, and candlelight to surprise him the night he died."

Ripples of anguish washed over her as he gave the accurate, never discussed before, play by play of that fatal night.

"He says you were upset because he was late getting home from work, and you went to bed." Cameron watched her with remorseful eyes.

"Mark says you forgot to blow out the candles. You would have died. He saved you from the fire." His horrified gaze fell to the faded, raised scaring on her thighs and upper right arm. "Oh my God, Vannah, it wasn't your fault. He died saving you because he loved you. He doesn't blame you."

He rushed over to her as she slid from the silk chaise to her knees, sobbing with despair. He eased her up, took her into his arms, and held her tight as she wept.

"It was my fault. I killed him. I'm so sorry, oh God, I didn't want to live after that night." She clung to his neck.

"There's something else." His hushed words calmed her

somewhat. "He wants one night with you."

"What?" Her face deadened with shock. "What does that mean?"

"Oh, God, how do I say this without getting slapped?" He let go and stepped back, sitting on the king-sized bed.

"What does he mean? What does Mark want?"

"Don't get mad, okay?"

"What?" She ran her trembling fingers across her face, clearing away the tears.

"In the mausoleum, he—" he shrugged as she flinched, "—that was him. I've never done this before, and the thought of it scares the crap out of me."

"What?" Vannah kneeled in front of him. The smell of roses grew stronger.

"I can channel spirits. He wants to use my—body, for one more night with you."

Vannah grew numb trying to take in what he suggested, in awe. "Cameron?"

"I swear to God, I'm not scamming you."

"I know you're not. It's confusing, though. You look nothing like him. I can't even imagine...."

"I'll make you a deal, okay?" His determined voice held her attention. "I've never channeled before because the thought of giving control away scares me, but Mark's spirit, he's aching for you. I'll be the conduit and let him communicate through me, and you do whatever you need or want. At least then he'll have had a chance to give you closure so he can go in peace."

"I don't understand."

"Spirits that linger and haunt are often here because of unfinished business, unresolved issues. They don't go to the white light and cross over. He's been waiting for you, all this time. You're his unfinished business Vannah. Your remorse, your guilt—he wants to ease your pain."

"I don't know what to say."

She was torn. What was the one wish anyone would have when they lost a loved one? Just one more time, one more hug, one more

I love you. Believing everything he said was a given. No one knew her feelings of guilt. The thought of speaking to Mark—being with him—through the body of another man was insane and dark, but tempting.

"Thank you." She nodded.

"Just for the record, though—" He smiled.

"What?"

"If all this hadn't happened, I would have been very...ecstatic to have had this one night with you myself. You're gorgeous."

"You're not so bad yourself, Adonis." She smirked.

"Huh?"

"Never mind."

Cameron gave her a wink and lay back. After a few minutes, his body went limp. He appeared asleep then jolted upright with his eyes open. His face appeared different, somehow, his posture—he didn't look like Cameron anymore.

"Savannah?" Tears trickled down his bronzed cheeks.

"Mark?" Vannah got up to her knees and moved toward him. His irises had changed; they had brown and green flecks now, no longer azure blue.

"Mark, is it you?" She threw her arms around his neck, squeezing tight.

"Savannah." He sobbed and grabbed hold of her, not letting go.

"Say something only you would know about me, please. I need to be sure."

"Baby doll, I miss cuddling with your feet, and you make a mean French toast, pretty lady."

Hysterical laughter exploded from her lips as she wept and giggled at the same time. Vannah cupped his cheeks and took in his face—it was Mark's and yet it wasn't.

"I'm so sorry, Mark, I should have—"

"Hush now, baby." He pressed a finger to her lips. "It wasn't your fault. It's just the way things were supposed to happen."

"Oh God." She pulled him close, clinging to his neck and kissed his cheeks.

"I don't have long, but I need to tell you something." He

grasped her arms and held her back far enough to capture her gaze.

"What?"

"I needed you to know, the time we had together was the best part of my life. I couldn't have asked for more. I was happy, and I love you so much."

Vannah's throat constricted and the muscles in her lips spasmed as she tried to hold back the building sobs.

"Enough tears sweetheart." He ran his thumbs across her cheeks, brushing away the wetness. "You've shed too many over me, for far too long. It's time to move on."

"Move on?" She shook her head with disbelief. "You're here now."

"Savannah, you are a young, beautiful woman with such a bright light. I can't bear to be the cause of it dimming so much. I need you to let me go. Let go of the guilt, the shame, and the regret."

As if by magic, she regained control of her emotions and her body again. The tears stopped, and her throat relaxed as she breathed a little easier.

"I can't explain how, but this night, this trip, this date, was all part of helping you heal. I wouldn't have done anything different that night, or any other night with you. I have no regrets, but one."

"What?" She watched him.

"My sole regret is not being able to get through to you sooner, to let you know."

"What?" A residual whimper rippled through her lungs.

"Your search since I died. Your ghost hunting expeditions. You were searching for proof, connection. This man...." He gestured to Cameron's body. "He's the only one you were around who could hear or see me."

"Those things that happened last night, the cold, the sound in my ear—"

"The smell of the old garden moss roses we planted in front of the house? Yes, that was all me trying to get your attention. It wasn't easy. You ignored everything I did to make you sense me."

"Well, there was a particular part I couldn't ignore." Vannah's cheeks grew warm.

"I couldn't resist."

"I didn't mind." A wave of giddiness rippled through her chest. "What happens now, Mark?"

Consuming her with his presence, he cradled her face in his hands. "I want to savor every last second with you."

She closed her eyes, listening to his words, feeling the heat of his palms on her cheeks. "Kiss me?"

His warm, moist mouth descended into a tender, slow-building, passionate kiss that made her toes curl.

"Oh, God, it is you." She focused on the sensations, the trail of his finger across her lips, along her neck, and down her chest. The muscles in her body responded to the gentle caresses with familiar intensity.

"I need you to know, I'm okay with this."

"With what?" She stared at him, no longer lost in his touch.

"I'm okay with you being with him, now, tonight, for as long as you want or need."

"With *him*?" She backed away, confused and a little upset he would feel that way.

"Baby, he was willing to give me his body so I could be with you. He's a good man. It wouldn't be right for me to stay any longer or to take advantage of the gift he offers. I've said and done what was needed."

"You won't stay? You won't be with me once more?" Her lips quivered with her despair.

"As much as I want to, it would be wrong."

"Why?" Her anger started to surface.

"Because, it won't help you let go, Savannah. It would give you false hope, leaving you still clinging to my memory. It would be selfish of me to get what I want and leave you grieving for me all over again. No, it's time."

"Mark."

"I love you Savannah Grace Teale. I will always love you. Promise me something?"

With knitted brows and frowning lips, she nodded.

"Promise me you'll make the most out of this life? You'll love unconditionally, you'll laugh often, and you'll embrace faith to get you through the rough times. You spent three years rejecting hope and trying to prove something you never believed to begin with. Life is too short to waste on regrets about things we can't change. The past is over and done with. Live in the here and now."

A calm she hadn't felt since his death spread through her racing mind. "I promise, Mark. I love you so much." She choked out the words. "Thank you for all the love you gave me. Thank you for the laughter." Another welling tear spilled down her cheek.

"I do have one more favor to ask?"

"What?"

"This guy, Cameron, give him a break, okay?"

"What do you mean?"

"All us ghosts have wreaked havoc on his sex life. This body is starving for satisfaction." He laughed and pointed down at his bulging pants. "As ready as a teenager. I'm not kidding."

Vannah burst out laughing with a few sobs entrenched. "Okay, baby. I'll do my best."

He collected the last tear with his thumb and watched her with tenderness. "It's time for me to go now." He pulled her close, and gripped her in a desperate and compelling manner. He claimed her lips one last time, unyielding as she melted.

Savoring every sensation of the exquisite and bitter-sweet bliss of her final moment with the man she thought she would spend the rest of her life with, Vannah cherished the lingering taste of his kiss, the softness of his sweeping tongue, and the last feeling of him holding her face. Lost in his embrace, she gasped when his body jerked and he pulled back.

"Vannah?" Cameron's body slumped over, out of his control. He felt as though his spine were jelly. *Now I know why I've never channeled before, and why I'm never doing it again.*

"It's okay." She eased him back onto the bed and tucked a pillow under his head. From the side of his vision, he caught a quick glimmer of white and then the room grew a little brighter. He drew a deep breath, trying to get the feeling back into his chest and lungs. The fragrance of roses—pervasive all evening—had disappeared.

"He's gone now." Vannah lay down beside him, resting her head on his chest as she caressed his stomach in tender swirls with her trembling fingers, a little sniff the only sign of any distress.

What little sensation he had, began tingling at the touch of her finger.

"Thank you, Cameron."

He tried to sit up, but felt like bricks were strapped to his back and he collapsed back onto the pillow.

"Oh man, my body feels like it weighs a million pounds." He patted down his shirt and pants, as he inspected himself. He'd blacked out and couldn't recall anything from the instant he let Mark into his body until this very moment.

"Did he...I mean did we...?" He searched his memory for any inkling of the events that had just unfolded. His mind was a blank page. It frustrated him. His body could have been in ecstasy, but he would never know it.

"We said good-bye. Nothing happened."

"You didn't—we—didn't?" He stammered. A hint of relief began to set in.

"You gave me a gift, Cameron." Vannah propped herself up on her right elbow and looked down into his eyes with the warmth of her brown gaze consuming him.

"What was that?" The stunning creature seemed to glow as she smiled at him.

"I'm feeling at peace for the first time since Mark's death. Because of what you did for me—us tonight, I know now that I can move on, guilt-free." Smiling, she traced her fingers across his lips.

"Vannah, What are you doing?" A blissful feeling washed over him with her slightest touch, but Cameron knew she just let go of the love of her life. After three years of mourning, should he even consider pursuing his desires?

"Okay, I lied, something did happen."

"What?" He checked his clothing again. His heart started to pound—he still couldn't remember anything. "You mean we did have—I mean, you had sex?"

"No, I let him go, and I promised to move on and make the most out of life."

"You did, huh?" The feeling of control began to come back a little at a time, first through his fingers, then his toes, feet and hands.... A sense of relief brought a smile to his face as he watched her.

"Yeah, I did," she purred. "He asked a personal favor, too."

"What's that?" Cameron brushed a soft wisp of curly flaxen hair from her face.

"He asked me to cut you some slack, you know, because of all the ghosts messing up your dates and all."

Cameron smirked, shaking his head, and dropped it back onto the pillow. "Wow, so now what?" Giving a grin, he got her non-verbal response.

She smiled and trailed her finger along his jaw, down his throat, and to his tightened chest. A deep throbbing sensation took over his chest and shoulders with a brief shudder.

"What's so funny?" Gaining control of his arms, he raised his hand and brushed his fingers along her exposed shoulders and arms, admiring her milky smooth skin.

"I'm not so sure the ghost did you such a big favor." She gave her words a low, sultry tone.

"Why not?"

"Let's just say, I have three years of suppressed sexuality to catch up on. You're in for a bumpy ride, sweetheart."

Vannah leaned over and lowered her lips to his, brushing them with a tease. Cameron inched up to meet her and she pulled back a little with a sassy smirk.

"How heavy does your body feel now?" She glanced down below his waist.

"Uh—"

"Don't worry, I can work with it." She giggled and descended upon his welcoming lips.

Vannah delved the tip of her tongue into the depths of his mouth, sweeping inside with tenderness. Cameron's palms cradled her warm face, pulling her closer to him. The delectable sweetness of her lips was intoxicating.

A jolt of elation shot through him as she eased herself up, sliding one leg over his torso and climbed on top of his rock hard bulge. Kissing with fervor, she moved her hips in a circular motion, rubbing against the clothing that separated them, feeling the warmth of her wetness on his hardness pushing up to her.

Grabbing his hands from her face, she guided them down to her voluptuous breasts, kneading and cupping them. She gripped the edge of her plunging neckline and pulled it down, allowing her rounded, perfect breasts to spill out for his worship. Cameron's fingers caught her erect peaks and pressed and twirled them into a maddening hardness.

"Oh you are so hot," he groaned, squeezing her fleshy mounds with growing intensity.

"Cameron?"

"Yeah." He welcomed her soft little kisses, seeking more with his lips.

"Tell me what you want?" She hummed into his ear then blazed a trail of famished kisses along his throat, finding her way back to his eager mouth.

"Oh—I want to get inside you."

"Tell me more." She hummed, sucking and licking his chin with gentle swirls.

"I wanna feel your tightness around me."

"Oh yes." She sat up and lifted her arms. Cameron sat with her in his lap and tugged the fragile zipper down the back of her dress. He inched the garment up her thighs, past her curvy hips, and pulled it over her head and off her arms, tossing it onto the bed.

"Oh, this is nice." He caressed the black lace that clung to her athletic, firm body.

"I'm glad you like it." He suckled along her throat and down across her exposed flesh. "Now, take it off, Cameron." She guided one of his hands down the length of her body to the heat between her legs. Her breath quickened as his fingers unhooked the teddy, revealing her moist, inviting mound.

Cameron eased the sheer material up, over her head, tossing it to the other side of the bed and wrapped his arms around the small of her back, pulling her closer to his mouth as his lips traveled across her warm flesh.

Running the tips of her nails over the planes of his back, Vannah grabbed the bottom of his shirt, inched it up over his head, and watched him with a smirk as she held it to the side and dropped it.

"Feeling better now?" She trailed her fingers along his arms, his shoulders, and down his chest and abdomen, sizing up his body. She wiggled her hips, pushing down as she ground her pelvis against his engorged cock.

"I think I'm recovering nicely, thanks." Traveling lips skimmed her chest, sought out her jutted nipples. His questing tongue swirled around her rosy peaks while he grasped her tight ass with kneading fingers.

"Any chance you're feeling a little adventurous?" he asked, lifting his mouth from her flesh. She entangled her fingers in his hair, pushing her breast deeper into his mouth.

"Adventurous? What did you have in mind?" She glided her hips back and forth, rubbing her clit against his hardness.

Cameron eased Vannah up. They stood facing one another beside the bed as he freed himself from the restriction of his pants and grabbed her by the waist, pressing against her. He reveled in the sensation of her hardened nipples brushing against his bare chest. He pulled her knee up against his hip. Vannah huffed with excitement, when he rubbed his stiffness against her trembling thigh. He eased her shoe off and released her leg, grabbing the other and doing the same.

He grabbed her by the wrist, plastering another rushed round of kisses over her mouth and neck then whisked her toward the patio door.

"What?" She gasped as he slid the glass entrance open. He swept her up into his arms and kissed her again strolling across the threshold.

☘

The warm summer air grazed against her tingling flesh as it brought with it, the exquisite nocturnal sounds of frogs and crickets singing filling the night air. Vannah drew back and watched the bright light of the harvest moon surrounded by glowing stars throughout the sky. The sound of rushing water grew loud as he moved across the massive rooftop patio toward an extravagant gazebo with an intriguing column of steam rising toward the sky. The rooftop was ablaze with candlelight and brought a luxurious serenity to her pulsating body.

"Oh, this is heaven," she moaned as he eased her feet first into the heated, bubbling water and she grasped his neck tighter, kissing deeper and harder with each breath. His lips didn't leave hers as he stepped over the edge, lowered himself into the hot tub, and guided her on top of him. He rubbed the tip of his steely hard on across her clit and she tried to lower herself onto him, but he held her hips up, just teasing her with the head. Vannah leaned back, examining his taunting smile.

"So it's like that is it?" she challenged with laughter.

"No, it's like this." He tangled her damp hair around his fingers and steered her to his lips while his other hand eased between her thighs, massaging the outer folds of her throbbing flesh. She felt her way down the length of his stomach seeking out his well-endowed offering and stroked him with slippery ease.

"Oh you're gonna get it."

"I'm counting on it." She bit his lower lip, then slid her tongue into his mouth and retreated again.

Cameron's gaze shot ripples of eager anticipation through her body. A jittery breath slipped out of her mouth when he yanked her hips closer to him and brought her down onto the head of his cock. Vannah grabbed his shaft and positioned it, easing her swollen folds open. Her heart was pounding and her breathing shaky as she descended, feeling the tip glide into her tightness. He tugged her down hard, filling her and impaling her. The heat of the jetting water felt cool against her skin in comparison to the pulsing blood coursing through her veins. Her face grew hot as she panted with sheer exhilaration.

"Oh, God, you're so tight."

The muscles in her thighs tensed as she moved up and down, reveling in her ultra-sensitive head-to-toe-shimmers of delight. Cameron gripped the crook of her hips while his fingertips dug into her flesh, pulling her onto him repeatedly, wild and driving. With each slamming thrust, water splashed out around them onto the ground and the waves rocked violently, propelled by their frantic motion.

A growing ripple of spasms erupted in her core as his thick cock chafed against her rigid inner wall. The repeated gyrating against her G-spot brought more intensity with every thrust, her muscles tightened, she clenched her mound around his thrusting cock, tensing and releasing.

"I'm almost, don't stop, don't stop—"she pushed down harder and faster onto him.

"That's it, Vannah, come for me." He slammed into her as he slipped a hand between her legs with skill and precision and massaged her hardened nub, while his other arm wrapped around her waist, still guiding the forceful rhythm of her movement onto him. The blissful sensation magnified with every flick of his finger and every ram.

"Come for me. Vannah."

"Yes, yes, I'm—uh—I'm—oh God," she shrieked. The rippling spasms exploded into a volcanic wave of shuddering ecstasy. Her body jerked with delight and her muscles stiffened, then released as waves of splendor rushed through her core, and spread over her quivering body.

"Ah yeah, I can feel you coming." His triumphant voice rang out, his breathing jagged in her ear as he laid his head back, swiveling his hips against her pulsing pussy.

Her throbbing clit sent more spasms as he gripped her swollen mound. Vannah eased up and off of his rock hard cock and guided him to stand facing her with his dark purple head swaying in front of her panting lips.

"I want you to come in my mouth."

"Oh yeah, suck my cock," he groaned, as she wrapped her shaking hand around his shaft and took his thick tip between her lips. A deep, masculine groan built in the bottom of his throat and roared out. She took him deep into her mouth and devoured him with desperation. She slid his pulsating hardness in and out of her mouth, caressing and cupping his balls while she sucked wildly.

"Oh you're fuckin' amazing." The strength of his hands gripping her head excited her as he thrust into her mouth. Her fingers found their way past his balls and massaged that elusive magic place between his cock and his ass, pressing into his flesh.

"Holy shit Vannah, that feels so good."

She worked the spot with her finger, still kneading his sack. Elated at the sound of his jagged breathing, she took the length of his cock deep into her throat and glided back and forth, huffing between strokes and sucking with insistence.

"Uh—Vannah—I'm ready to come." He gasped pulling her head closer. "Uh yeah—uh yeah—here it comes—oh fuck—"

She eagerly welcomed the warm, salty fluid as it spewed into her throat. Cameron's body stiffened in release.

"Uh—uh—" Vannah felt his body shudder. Cameron gripped her hair, pulling her off his cock. She stood up facing him.

His smoldering, insatiable stare sent a spasm through her core. She didn't resist when he yanked her to his mouth, and kissed her hard and deep, gasping between kisses.

"You're amazing." He braced himself, dropping back into the hot tub seat.

Vannah sat down onto his lap again, kissing his neck and his cheeks then trailing her way back to his panting lips.

"So, how's that for three years of catching up?"

"Oh, Cameron." She shook her head.

"What?" He gave a worried stare.

"I told you, three years of repressed sexuality. Honey, I'm just getting started; I said you were in for a bumpy ride." She giggled, reaching down and stroking his semi-hardness again.

"Wow, what a woman." He grinned. "How about a cool

shower? We don't want to get a fever, do we?"

"Maybe a little room service, dipping chocolate—we've got all night." Vannah traced her tongue along the outside of his lips in a sultry manner.

"Let's go." Cameron jumped to his feet.

"As ready as a teenager." She laughed, eying his hard on.

"What?"

"Nothing Adonis, but do me a favor?" She stood up and cradled his handsome face.

"What's that, madam?—uh—I mean miss?" Cameron gave a sly smirk at her challenging stare.

"Uh huh." She smiled. "Will you be sure to blow out all these candles? Please?" She glanced around at the dozens of flickering flames. She might have been over the past, but she wouldn't forget its lessons as she forged into her future.

"With pleasure, Miss Savannah." His drawl sent shivers up her spine.

~ABOUT THE AUTHOR~

When Kali Willows isn't busy being the married mother of two, certified trainer or counselor extraordinaire, she is shadowing worlds of paranormal passion & intrigue. Her goal in life? She has many, but her writing goal is creating emotional, compelling stories and characters you can't help but love, hate and cheer for.

A good cup of tea with the crackling fire gets her creative juices flowing in the wee hours of the night, when the house is quiet and she can type away to her heart's desire. Writing short stories and poems since her preteens, she has entered into the powerful world of paranormal romance writing, and constructing new worlds for her readers to explore and indulge in.

Now a multi-published author, Kali has also hosted her own Blogtalkradio show; "Between Moonlit Covers," and loves every aspect of the entertainment industry. Passionate about writing in a variety of venues, Kali aspires to bring some of her riveting stories to the big screen.

Being somewhat unorthodox, Kali took her ambition to please her readers to a completely new level, and created an online survey for them to fill out. She gave her readers the opportunity to decide what her next story is going to be; the characters, plot, setting and many other elements. The intention is, to give them what they want in a story, and Kali loves a writing challenge. Who knows, it may just inspire the next bestseller!

Visit Kali online at:
www.kaliwillows.com

www.ingramcontent.com/pod-product-compliance
Lightning Source LLC
Chambersburg PA
CBHW051456170626
46811CB00002B/510